OF VINES AND VICTIMS

PHILLIPA NEFRI CLARK

Storm
PUBLISHING

This is a work of fiction. Names, characters, businesses, places, events and incidents are either the products of the author's imagination or used in a fictitious manner. Any resemblance to actual persons, living or dead, or actual events is purely coincidental.

Copyright © Phillipa Nefri Clark, 2026

The moral right of the author has been asserted.

All rights reserved. No part of this book may be reproduced or used in any manner without the prior written permission of the copyright owner. This prohibition includes, but is not limited to, any reproduction or use for the purpose of training artificial intelligence technologies or systems.

To request permissions, contact the publisher at rights@stormpublishing.co

Ebook ISBN: 978-1-83700-096-8
Paperback ISBN: 978-1-83700-097-5

Cover design: Diane Meacham
Cover images: Shutterstock

Published by Storm Publishing.
For further information, visit:
www.stormpublishing.co

ALSO BY PHILLIPA NEFRI CLARK

Temple River

The Cottage at Whisper Lake

The Bookstore at Rivers End

The House at Angel's Beach

The Secrets of Willow Bay

The Lost Girl of Seahaven

A Travelling Celebrant Mystery

Of Marriage and Murder

Of Funerals and Feuds

Of Retreats and Revenge

Rivers End Romantic Women's Fiction

The Stationmaster's Cottage

Jasmine Sea

The Secrets of Palmerston House

The Christmas Key

Taming the Wind

Martha

Detective Liz Moorland Series

Lest We Forgive

Lest Bridges Burn

Lest Tides Turn

Lest Nobody Lives

Lest Angels Weep

Last Known Contact

Charlotte Dean Mysteries

Christmas Crime in Kingfisher Falls

Book Club Murder in Kingfisher Falls

Cold Case Murder in Kingfisher Falls

Plans for Murder in Kingfisher Falls

Festive Felony in Kingfisher Falls

Bindarra Creek Rural Fiction

A Perfect Danger

Tangled by Tinsel

Doctor Grok's Peculiar Shop Short Story Collection

Simple Words for Troubled Times

To those who touch our hearts

PROLOGUE

Broad daylight was meant to be the safest time to be out and about. Never more than on a pleasantly warm day when people should be enjoying the weather, visiting the beautiful parklike grounds of the winery to taste the latest offerings or ordering a picnic lunch to eat by the small lake. A day just like today.

Yet there wasn't a soul in sight as Daphne Jones ran as fast as her legs would go, veering off a path to weave between trees in the hope she could throw off her pursuer.

Heart thudding a million miles an hour, she threw herself against the trunk of a massive old oak.

One, one thousand. Two, one thousand. Three, one thousand... oh dear.

Hiding behind a tree and counting reminded her of childhood games of hide and seek.

Well, this was hide and seek but far removed from being a game. Not when the person seeking her was a killer!

As the heaving of her chest lessened, Daphne listened. Somewhere in the distance, a horse whinnied. Somewhere closer, a peal of laughter carried from up near the Crystal Springs restaurant. And much closer, a twig snapped.

There was no time to make a plan. Daphne took off again, this time in a straight line to the only place left to hide. Trees weren't doing the job and she knew she had no chance of outrunning the person who was on her trail. Running was not Daphne's thing and even though the only people she knew for sure were around to help were near the restaurant, that was up the hill. A steep hill.

She raced through the huge open doors of the heart of the winery... the massive barrel hall where wine casks stretched as far as the eye could see. The biggest of these were the stainless steel vats at the furthest end, towering over mere humans. Perfect to hide behind.

Rather than career down the middle of the building in plain sight, Daphne ducked down the first aisle to the right which was lined with barrels which were still a decent size. But in here she had a new issue. As much as she adored her cute pumps with their low, block heel, the shoes were tapping far too loudly on the concrete floor. At the end of the aisle she stopped and slipped them off. The ground was cold but easy enough to walk on and at least she was quiet now. Or would be once she caught her breath.

Finally reaching the large barrels at the edge of the room Daphne found a narrow walkway running between them and the thick stone wall. The gloom forced her to slow to a shuffle until she figured she was about halfway along.

Surely from here she wouldn't be seen if she sent a text message?

Her mind was a whirlwind of thoughts tangled up with the events of the last few minutes. A simple conversation in a carpark. An offhand comment which suddenly poured light onto what was supposed to be a closed case. And the wrong choice of direction forcing Daphne away from help.

She pulled her phone from a pocket and made sure it was on silent mode before typing a message to John and sending it. And then two more to the other people who might see it if he didn't. In the moment or two in which her phone screen lit up around her, she realised there was a door just a bit further along.

If I can open it, then I can sneak out.

'Mrs Jones.'

Daphne jumped and almost dropped her phone.

The voice echoed. How close was he?

'There's no way out.'

Oh, yes there is.

She edged closer to the door.

'We might as well have a face-to-face conversation. Come to an agreement.'

With a killer? Not likely.

His voice was closer and a flashlight lit the end of the narrow walkway. But Daphne was at the door now, her fingers reaching for the handle.

'It doesn't have to be this way. Daphne. May I call you that?'

As if she'd answer such a question. Everyone called her Daphne or Daph or even Auntie Daph. But not him. She pushed the handle down. It didn't move much. Then up. The same. It must be locked.

Her legs were shaking from all the running and probably the adrenaline. If she had to run more... he might just catch her. And if she tried climbing the ladder up the side of the steel vat?

Was she about to end up drowning in red wine?

ONE

EARLIER THAT WEEK

The road was as straight as any Daphne Jones had ever travelled and to be completely honest, it was quite boring. On either side the landscape was flat. Not in a pretty way with interesting hills in the distance and the occasional river or green paddocks with horses, but sparse and vacant and dry. As for the road? Well, there hadn't been so much as a curve for kilometres. Straight and flat.

'As a pancake.'

'Is that what you want for breakfast, doll?'

Daphne glanced at her husband, John, who was driving.

'Oh dear, did I say that aloud? But now you mention it, I am getting a bit hungry.'

They'd been up before dawn, leaving their overnight camping site behind with the intention of reaching their destination by early afternoon. Their caravan made life on the road so easy but Bluebell did slow them down as well, not to mention their regular stops at any places of interest, and they did like to browse when visiting places.

'We've not even had a coffee yet, thanks to a certain someone wanting to get on the road especially early, but the GPS tells me there's a town about twenty minutes away, so what if we stop and find somewhere to eat?'

Their new car – a hybrid SUV – was a dream. Not only more environmentally friendly and economical to run, but it had so many bells and whistles. Like the GPS screen. It had done Daphne out of the job she least enjoyed on their trips: navigation.

'I like that idea. I just can't imagine a town suddenly appearing out of nowhere, though.'

John chuckled. 'It is a bit like we're in the middle of nowhere.'

They were travelling across the middle of Victoria – roughly. The drive was under three hundred kilometres but through all kinds of terrain, from the current monotonous landscape to twisty roads, hilly regions, and everything in between. Their destination was a town not far from the beautiful vineyard and winery where Daphne would officiate a wedding this Saturday. Her fourth in as many weeks.

'We've never been to Benalla, have we, dear?' She didn't wait for an answer. 'We've driven past it of course, or at least the exit from the highway, but not gone into the town. And no reason why we should; we don't even know anyone who lives here, apart from the happy couple. And even that has just been email contact with the prospective groom.'

'Well, we don't usually know anyone. Other than a couple of our friends' weddings you've officiated.'

This was true. Everyone else Daphne had officiated for had been strangers – usually ones who'd found her business through a search engine. Occasionally from word of mouth. Usually it worked well.

Goodness, Daph. Why are you so negative?

'They sound like a lovely couple from what you've told me.'

At least John hadn't noticed her mood.

'Indeed!' She reached for a notebook covered in pictures of wedding bells which was in her oversized handbag. Talking about weddings was much more interesting than the current landscape. 'Let me see.' She turned to the notes she'd made for the trip. This system worked well – keeping dot points, names, details of anything important, and her meandering thoughts in one place. Of course, she had a lot more stored on her laptop, as well as the formal wedding book she kept.

The car slowed as John braked to give a mob of kangaroos room to hop across the road up ahead. By the time they reached the crossing point, the fifty or so roos were disappearing across the flat plain.

'So, on Saturday I'll be officiating the wedding of Arvin and Belle. Arvin and *Anna*belle.'

John glanced her way with a questioning look.

'When the query first appeared through my website my heart skipped a beat and I thought... well, hoped...' As familiar silly tears prickled at the back of her eyes, Daphne blinked a few times and kept reading. 'Of course it isn't her. The paperwork has a different surname. And surely if it was our Annabelle, she'd have been in touch herself instead of her fiancé doing it all alone?'

'He's done all the planning?'

'Unsure, but certainly all the communication so far has been with him. More often than not the bride will be the main contact – although more and more it seems a shared process – but I don't believe I've had even one direct contact with this Annabelle. Belle.' She corrected herself and glanced at the book. 'The wedding is being held at the Crystal Springs winery, which is owned by the groom's family.'

'You've not officiated a wedding at a winery before.'

'Just about everywhere else, love. Beaches, parks hidden in valleys, private homesteads, and even a Christmas tree farm! I've written up a schedule based on my emails with the groom. Tomorrow I'll meet with the happy couple to go over the ceremony and we're both invited to dinner at the winery restaurant. Then there's two days for me to finesse the ceremony and incorporate any last-minute changes before the wedding on Saturday.'

'And then we'll have a few days' break afterwards to explore the area.'

Daphne gazed out of the window. She loved travelling with John and Bluebell. Loved officiating weddings and, occasionally, helping mourners with a funeral or goodbye ceremony. But lately she had been missing home. Their caravan had everything they needed... except their friends.

As if sensing her thoughts, John reached over and squeezed her leg. 'And then we'll go back to Rivers End for a while. As the season turns to autumn and there's fewer weddings, it seems the ideal time to return to our other life.'

'Yes. Yes, it does, John.'

She sighed but now it was without the melancholy. Every couple deserved the best and this might not be the wedding of *their* Annabelle, but Daphne would ensure the bride and groom had a wedding to remember.

It was just after one when Bluebell was carefully backed into her spot for the next few days.

After staying at so many camping sites, Daphne knew John's routine. He'd unshackle Bluebell and move the car then go through a long list of checks to make sure the caravan was safe and in good condition. He was pedantic about it and there was no rushing the man, so Daphne went for a quick walk to check out the camping ground.

At least that helped distract her from the growling in her stomach. No more leaving before dawn without some food and a cup of coffee, because relying on small towns to feed them had been a disaster! They'd only managed to buy a chocolate bar each when they'd stopped at the town John had mentioned, because the only café was closed, so they'd had to keep going until reaching their destination.

This camping ground was set right on Lake Benalla, a tranquil body of water virtually in the middle of Benalla. There were only a handful of sites in this quiet little spot and what set this one apart from most camping grounds was the lack of amenities. It was all about enjoying nature and being self-sufficient.

Which is why we have Bluebell. Our little home away from home.

Daphne turned back. From the short distance she'd walked, Bluebell shone like a beacon with her bright blue and white paint. So pretty. And as John wandered into view, she stopped for a moment, unable to keep a smile off her face.

I'm the luckiest woman in the world.

Intent on his checklist, her husband didn't notice her. John kept a clipboard with all sorts of information about the car and the caravan, as well as his regular 'arrival' and then 'departure' lists.

John was her high-school sweetheart and she loved him today as much – actually, more – than the day she'd said 'I do'. His generosity and easy-going nature was a good match for her kind heart and occasional impulsiveness. They never argued. And they shared many interests.

'All good to go inside,' he called out now.

She hurried over. 'Lovely. First things first. A nice cup of tea.'

'Any chance of a sandwich? Or anything edible, really.'

He looked so hopeful that Daphne kissed his cheek in passing. 'There's leftover pasta which I can heat up in as long as it takes to boil the kettle.'

Climbing into Bluebell was like coming home. When John originally found the small caravan, it had been little more than a shell. Lovingly restored, she now included a modern kitchenette and bathroom, comfortable sleeping quarters, and a practical living area. It took no time at all to heat two bowls of macaroni cheese and make a pot of their favourite tea and as Daphne placed everything onto the table, John stepped in, sniffing the air.

'Real food.'

Daphne grinned. She enjoyed cooking and even if she said so herself, was pretty good at it. Apart from cookies. For a long time she'd baked them in volume, forcing everyone around her to eat the chewy or crunchy round offerings without realising how kind and tolerant people were. It took a couple of rather nasty women at a celebrant conference who didn't care if they hurt Daphne's feelings to discover her tasty cookies were... not very tasty.

John sat and reached for the teapot. 'Nice to see that smile back. Shall I pour?'

After lunch, John couldn't wait to see what the fishing was like. They'd chosen this camping park because of its reputation for the hobby which John enjoyed. He also loved photography, and was becoming quite an expert at family histories.

Daphne sat beneath the awning and watched him wander in the direction of the water, fishing pole and tackle in one hand and a stool in the other.

When they'd first decided to pursue her dream of being a travelling celebrant, Daphne had worried that John might be bored. After all, he'd been a busy and successful real estate agent for decades. But all it took was their first trip away to calm her nerves. He loved being out on the road and didn't mind living in the small confines of Bluebell one bit.

'How did you get so lucky, Daph?' she sighed aloud.

John would be a couple of hours, no doubt, which gave her a chance to look over her notes and begin to pull everything together for the big event on Saturday.

She opened her laptop and inserted a dongle in order to get internet access. Some camping grounds provided Wi-Fi but not here, where there wasn't so much as a shower block. While she waited for the laptop to do its thing, Daphne opened a folder on the home page. As a couple who were unable to have children of their own, they'd chosen to foster for many years and inside the folder were beautiful reminders of the children who'd come into their lives.

Rather than lingering on each image, she went directly to those of the only foster child they'd lost contact with. Although every child was precious and an important part of their lives, one had touched Daphne unlike any other. Annabelle.

She'd arrived at their home as a nine-year-old who was afraid of the world until a loving home environment and the magic of Rivers End helped her find confidence and a happy life. Over almost five wonderful years, Annabelle had thrived and the couple had done something they'd never done before. They began the process to adopt her.

But on Annabelle's fourteenth birthday there was a knock on the door and as quickly as she'd come into their lives, she was gone. Her biological father had been located and refused to sign adoption papers. Although he'd never been in her life, he fought for the right to take her home with him and all too soon the house was emptier than ever before.

Daphne helped herself to tissues. Her heart had been broken. And John's. Annabelle had been star-struck to meet her dad for the first time and she'd barely looked back.

Who could blame her? Losing her mum when she was only nine and then her dad comes along like a rock star with his nice car and promise of a pony.

The saddest thing wasn't welcoming another wonderful child into their home. It wasn't repainting Annabelle's room or starting over. It was the wait. The visits to the letterbox. Answering every phone call with a lift of the heart which was dashed.

She'd never been in touch.

Not once.

There were so many photographs, but one which Daphne particularly loved. Annabelle was celebrating her thirteenth birthday and was blowing out candles on a cake, with Daphne and John on either side. It was a moment when all three were smiling at the camera and it was as much a family shot as Daphne had ever seen. She touched the screen. Annabelle had rich red hair and a few freckles on her nose, bright green eyes and the cheekiest of smiles.

'I miss you, darling. Be happy.'

Her voice came out as a whisper and with a big sigh, Daphne

closed the folder. Having Annabelle in their lives for so long was a blessing and Daphne wished her every joy. Wherever she was.

TWO

Once John returned – empty handed for once but looking relaxed – they decided to explore the town. After Daphne had changed into the soft, loose pants and top she favoured and put on her walking shoes, they locked Bluebell and headed back the way they'd driven in, but on foot.

'Some towns just have a special appeal,' John said. He'd taken Daphne's hand in his. 'From the little we've seen I'd say Benalla is one of those places.'

'You just like having somewhere to fish and take photos within an easy walk of the shops,' Daphne teased. 'No distance to anything.'

'True. But we had that when we were staying in Little Bridges and I'm not certain I'm inclined to visit there again.'

'It was rather challenging.'

Something of an understatement because while the town itself was pleasant, there'd been two murders during their stay. Not to mention histrionics from the bride and a puzzle which was almost too hard to solve. And yet Daphne had.

'Well, you rose to the challenge, doll.'

'It would be nice to have an uneventful celebration this time!'

John chuckled. 'Couldn't agree more.'

They stopped to admire the library, which was built close to the lake.

'Might do some genealogy research while you're otherwise occupied.'

'It looks so nice. Modern but inviting.'

Next, they headed in the direction of the main road, where the traffic was surprisingly busy. Having lived in a small town for all their married life, both Daphne and John enjoyed the similarities – and the unique finds – yielded by their travels. For a while they wandered, window-shopping and taking note of places of interest for another day.

'Would you like to eat out tonight?'

'Quite honestly, I'd like to stay home tonight, if you don't mind. But I'd rather not cook.' The travelling had tired her more than usual. 'What if we look for a takeaway for later?'

'Sounds good. And I'm happy to walk back over to collect.'

They walked all the way down one side of the main street then back up the other, deciding to leave several side roads for another day. Before heading back, they popped into one of the supermarkets to get fresh milk, bread, and a few bits and pieces. John collected the free local newspaper from a wire basket out the front.

'Anything you fancy for dinner yet?' Daphne asked. 'I've picked up three takeaway menus so far.'

'Make that four.' He helped himself to one outside a pizza restaurant. 'Happy with any we've come across so far. But for now, I'd love another cup of tea.'

'There's an article in here about the wedding.' John turned the paper so Daphne could see. 'All about the winery as well.'

He was happy to sip his tea while Daphne peered at the page.

'Ooh... Did you see the picture?'

'Briefly.'

Outside the open doors of a large cellar, huge vats and barrels visible, a group of a dozen or so people huddled together, arms around each other, including a gentleman in a wheelchair. In front of them was a painted sign: BELLE & ARVIN. TWO HEARTS, ONE PERFECT LIFE.

Daphne read the caption aloud. 'Members of the Kingsley family and some of the bridal party gather to enjoy a glass of wine and admire the sign which will be part of the ceremony on Saturday. Anyone who has visited Crystal Springs will appreciate the natural beauty of the winery locally known as the pride of the town. The family has grown grapes and made award-winning wines on the land for several generations, with Arvin expected to take over as head winemaker in the future. Belle is the daughter of the owner of several liquor shops and a pub in the region, which makes for a perfect combination. A perfect life indeed.'

She turned the page back to John, who peered at the photograph.

'Looks like a nice group of people. A nice, friendly group.'

'So not a murderous group?' Daphne grinned when John's eyes shot up to hers. 'No sign of criminals? Bad guys hidden in plain sight?'

'Not even a little bit funny, Madam Celebrant Sleuth.'

But his lips twitched and his eyes sparkled.

'I have nothing but good feelings about this wedding, love, so don't stress. People are always happy at wineries so this event will be as relaxed and trouble-free as a wedding can be.'

'Any idea which are the bride and groom?' John offered the paper back to Daphne. 'No names are printed.'

She took another look. There were several younger men and women but nobody holding hands or clearly a couple. One of the women wore a baseball cap and it was a bit hard to see her face. Another young lady was heavily pregnant. None of them looked like she imagined Annabelle would and Daphne planted a smile on her face.

'So, what should we order for dinner?'

. . .

The winery was a few kilometres from town and John had already planned his spare time once Daphne was safely at her destination.

She'd scheduled an hour and a half with the bride and groom to talk about the ceremony; plenty of time for him to drive to the neighbouring town of Winton. He'd heard about a stunning mural painted at the local cemetery and hoped to get some good photos of it.

Daphne had been quiet through the drive until they'd turned onto the road where the winery was.

'Sometimes I wonder what I'm doing.'

Her words were quietly delivered and not at all like her usual self. John glanced at Daphne as she continued speaking.

'When you found my father... my biological father... it answered so many questions. I'll never forget you doing that for me, love. Plus I gained a cousin and his family.'

Up ahead, a large sign declared the entry to CRYSTAL SPRINGS WINERY & PINNACLE PESTAURANT. John pulled over and turned to Daphne. 'Why so pensive?'

'I don't know. Not really. You know I love my job. Love seeing people start their married lives together.'

'But?'

She sighed, a long, soft exhalation. Her eyes were just a little bit misty and he took her hand.

'Yesterday, I got the feeling you are missing home.'

'Missing our friends. And family.'

'We could easily swing by Shady Bend on the way back to Rivers End. Drop in on your dad and Constance and Adam.'

At last there was a smile. 'Would you mind?'

'Well, considering we just used the last of Constance's Secret Sauce, I think we owe it to ourselves to restock the pantry.' His fingers tightened. 'Let's do that. And in the meantime, you have a lovely ceremony to perform and a couple who chose you to do so. Be proud of that.'

'I am. Very.'

'How about you go and meet this bride and groom? Do what you do so well to make people happy.'

'I do love you, John Jones.'

'Goes both ways, my sweetheart.' He leaned over and gently kissed her lips. 'Hope that didn't mess up your lipstick.'

'Not even a bit.'

He nosed back onto the road and a moment later drove through a grand pair of open iron gates between two stone walls. A bitumen driveway wound through gum trees, past a lake – complete with a boathouse – then between seemingly endless rows of grapevines. The ground rose ahead and the driveway split into three.

'More big gates to the left and a "private residence" notice,' Daphne said. There was a signpost. CELLAR DOOR CARPARK IS TO THE RIGHT.

'So we go straight ahead into the restaurant's carpark.'

John slowed to enter a parking area for about fifty vehicles abutting the base of a steep hill. At its top was a long, low building.

'That must be Pinnacle, which is a perfect name for it,' Daphne said. 'I can't wait to see the view from up there.'

John pulled into a spot close to a series of stone steps.

'Right on time, love. Looks like I'm about to meet the bride and groom.' She climbed out of the car, leaning back in to collect her briefcase and handbag with a smile at John. 'Shall I message when I'm ready?'

'I'll only be about ten minutes aw—'

'Aunt Daphie? Aunt Daphie!'

The voice calling was female and excited. Daphne's eyes widened and she stepped back to straighten. John immediately undid his seat belt. Only one person had ever called her that. He pushed the door open, swinging his feet out and moving the minute they touched the ground.

'Oh! Uncle John!'

The young woman with the baseball cap – from the photo in the newspaper – was running down the path, followed at a more sedate pace by a young man who wore a huge grin. She came to a stop a few metres away, tears streaming down her face.

Daphne seemed speechless. Her hands reached out then dropped again.

Pulling the cap off, the younger woman released a cascade of red wavy hair.

'It's me, Auntie. Me, Uncle.'

'Annabelle?'

'You do remember me!'

Like a slow-motion movie, Daphne and John moved as one to the foster child they'd never forgotten, arms ready to hold her and leave behind the ache of sadness of more than a decade.

<h1 style="text-align:center">THREE</h1>

It was all Daphne could do not to sit on the ground and sob her heart out. Wrapping her arms around Belle and being squeezed back – *so* hard – was like a dream. Except, this was real. And John's face was a mirror of her emotions. Caught between joy and tears.

She finally stepped back and felt eyes on her. The young man had caught up and his smile was warm and genuine. He was a good-looking young man. Quite a bit taller than Daphne, with broad shoulders and dark brown hair which flopped over his forehead, he had a tissue and was wiping his cheeks. That almost undid the fragile hold she had on her feelings. But then he embraced her like an old friend.

'I'm Arvin. I can't believe this really happened the way I hoped. Thank you.'

'Thank me?'

John and Belle were having a quiet conversation.

Arvin took Daphne's arm and they moved a few steps away. 'I only told Belle half an hour ago.'

'Told her...?'

'The name of our celebrant.'

Oh... surely you didn't keep it from her?

'I took a chance. I'm not a risk taker and she might have reacted an entirely different way.'

'I'm not completely following you.'

'My concern was she'd veto my brainwave. You know, fall back on her fears and all the nonsense she's been told.' Arvin glanced at Belle, who had her arm through John's and was approaching. He lowered his voice. 'Just know she's always loved you.'

None of this was making sense. Belle was the bride-to-be. She had only just found out that Daphne was the celebrant. Arvin felt it was a risk... and those cryptic last words were a concern. She felt like her head was spinning from all the excitement and confusing information.

'It really is you, Aunt Daphie.' Belle gazed at her through wide green eyes. 'After all this time, you finally came to see me.'

'But I...' Daphne's heart sank. 'John and I never knew.'

Belle frowned and she looked at Arvin, who reached for her hand.

'We didn't know it was your wedding,' John added. 'Or where you live.'

'You didn't know?'

Arvin cleared his throat. 'My doing, babe. I didn't tell you or Daphne.'

Dropping his hand like it was burning her, Belle turned to Daphne. 'You had no idea you were booked to officiate my wedding? None at all?'

'Well, no. The information I have, including your birth certificate, is for Belle Boyd and when you lived with us you were called Annabelle Lawson.'

Tears filled Belle's eyes. 'You're only here because you didn't know it was me. Not because you wanted to see me again. I used to dream you'd come to one of my birthdays or even just send a card. But it was all just a job for you.' With a sob, she spun in the opposite direction and sprinted away.

'Wait!' Arvin made to follow but John rested a hand on his arm.

'Hold on a minute, son. Why would Belle believe we're only here because we had no idea it was our Annabelle?' His voice was calm but there was a waver in his words.

Daphne had no doubt he felt every bit as confused and upset as she did right now. And although her instinct was to follow Belle – who was fast disappearing into a wooded area – she wanted an explanation as well. There was a giant lump in her throat but somehow this all had to be sorted and hurt feelings fixed.

Arvin's face had reddened and he nodded. 'I messed up, didn't I? Thing is, Belle's been misled over the years. About the two of you.'

'Misled, how?' John asked.

'Her grandmother made up some story about foster parents not being allowed to stay in touch. That was when Belle first moved in with her dad and was desperate to call you. Her grandmother lived with them both until she passed away and was always telling Russell – that's Belle's dad – to keep the past in the past. She's why he'd turned his back on Belle's mum. And he just went along with it all to keep the peace.'

'But why would it have hurt for Belle to phone us?' Daphne squeaked the question.

'I've no idea and nor does Belle, and Russell claims he knew nothing about it. But she was homesick for you. However, as odd as the woman was, the grandmother genuinely loved Belle, almost on sight. Probably scared she'd lose her. Lots of dysfunction in the Boyd family.' He broke off and heaved a sigh. 'Please, I have to find her.'

'I'll go. Does she still like climbing trees?' Daphne was already on her way and called over her shoulder. 'You keep talking to John, please.'

Finding Belle was easy. It was a case of following the sound of her crying and it took all of Daphne's self-control not to simply throw her arms around the distressed young woman. But there was so much more to this unexpected reunion than she could get her head around yet and Belle would surely feel the same.

Small and careful steps, Daph.

When Belle had come to live with them, she'd picked a tree in the garden with low branches and made it her refuge when her emotions ran high. And as Daphne stepped around one lovely old oak, there she was, back to the trunk, legs against her chest and arms wrapped around them, perched on a solid bough. She was only just above Daphne's eye level.

At first Belle had her head buried against her raised knees and didn't see her, but after a moment, Daphne tentatively touched her arm.

Her head shot up and her body tensed as if she was going to jump down and run.

'Please stay. Please talk to me.' Daphne withdrew her hand and took a small step back to preserve Belle's personal space. 'Or at least let me talk.'

The silence dragged and then Belle brushed away the tears with both palms and nodded. She straightened her legs but made no move to climb down. This was a comfort to Daphne. Over the years they'd fostered her, Annabelle – Belle – had always been willing to listen. Even when her little heart was broken about her mum, she'd let Daphne or John rattle on about all manner of things and it would calm her. Reset her feelings.

Think about every word before you speak.

Daphne's hands were shaking but this had to count. Belle might not give her another chance.

'When I opened Arvin's query about booking me to celebrate your wedding, he mentioned his fiancée as Belle. And my heart skipped a beat. Do you know why?'

Belle shook her head.

'Every time I hear the name Annabelle or Belle, I hope... just for a heartbeat... it is you. When you went to live with your dad I used to check the letterbox twice a day in case there was a letter from you. A card. After a while John and I had a big talk and although we both missed you so much, we knew you were safe and hopefully happy in your new life.'

'How?'

'How did we know?'

Another nod.

'I *could* say that the government agency which oversaw your move to your father would have been present in your life for some time and ensured you were in a safe environment. Or I *could* say our one meeting with your dad gave John and me confidence in his sincere desire to bring you into his life.'

The doubt in Belle's eyes cut into Daphne's heart.

'The truth though is going to sound strange. I felt it in here.' Daphne touched her chest above her heart. 'I've always been sensitive to things which other people often laugh at, and I understand if you do as well, but some part of me just believed it was true.'

'Like an emotional connection. One we can never break.'

'Exactly.'

Swinging down from the branch, Belle stayed on the other side but her expression was thoughtful, rather than distressed. 'Arvin is the only person who knows this, but I feel stuff. Not mind-reading stuff but sometimes the breeze picks up when I'm walking and I almost hear a whisper in the wind. A good feeling that someone is thinking about me. And dreams really matter and I might think about one for days.'

'So you know in your heart I've never stopped loving you.' Daphne blinked to keep the tears at bay. 'As foster parents, John and I were bound by certain rules and privacy laws and never heard from your dad other than one phone call a week after you left which was to thank us for the years we cared for you. And darling, there was not even one day we didn't think about you. Seeing you now is my dream come true and I will always thank Arvin for making it happen, even if you... even if you send us away.'

In one quick motion, Belle ducked under the branch and had her arms around Daphne.

'I'm really torn, Auntie. I love you and Uncle John, but I love my dad and I hope we can work this all out.'

Daphne held her tightly, slightly rocking her as she'd done in the past when Belle was overwhelmed.

'There's so much going on.' Belle's head dropped onto her shoulder. 'The wedding arrangements. Dad's opinions and... his friends. And the problems with poor Arvin and his family.'

'What problems?' Releasing Belle, Daphne took a step back.

Belle sighed heavily. 'Crystal Springs almost had to be sold after his dad's accident and if it wasn't for community support then it would be long gone. It's only in the last year things have turned around but the strain has taken a toll on both of Arvin's parents. And he's so talented and everyone knows he'll become the next winemaker here once Claude retires, but...'

'But?'

'We think that Claude's been offered a job elsewhere. There's rumours but he denies it and just gets grumpy with Arvin when they work together.'

'Not pleasant.'

'It just feels like one more problem to deal with before the weekend.' Belle suddenly smiled. 'But you really are here. I can't believe I got so silly back in the carpark but it was a shock.'

'Serious question.' Daphne gazed at Belle. 'I have several dear friends who are wonderful celebrants and I'm happy to call them and see if one could come here on Saturday. If me being your celebrant is too much, I will... understand.' She added the last bit with a break in her voice. Marrying this couple meant more than she'd realised.

'Belle? Daphne?'

Arvin's voice drifted through the trees.

'I've worried everyone.'

'No, dear. You are a bride-to-be and have a million things stressing you. And it is as clear as day how much Arvin adores you.'

'And I adore you, Auntie. And I don't want anyone else on that podium but you.'

FOUR

John wasn't going anywhere after the surprise of seeing Annabelle again. Belle. Murals and photographs could wait, because this was one of those moments in time one would never forget.

The four of them sat around an outdoor table at the restaurant, drinking in incredible views of the surrounding landscape. Grape vines stretched in every direction, meadows with horses grazing, and even further away, a mountain range. The Great Dividing Range. They'd come here straight from the carpark, once Belle and Daphne had returned, both looking much happier. Arvin had suggested a coffee before they got started and everyone agreed.

'Where does the winery's land end?' John asked.

'Do you see the top of the hill to the right? There's a single tree on its top?' Arvin pointed. 'Everything on this side of the hill is ours and then,' his arm slowly swept to the left, 'it ends where the river forks. That's our boundary.'

John let out a low whistle of appreciation. 'So the horse paddocks are yours?'

Belle's face lit up. 'That is where we keep all the oldies and the rescues. Horses, ponies, and some donkeys.'

'Oh! You always said you wanted to be a caretaker of the less fortunate.' Daphne was peering in the direction of the meadows. 'So, you live here as well?'

'No, still with Dad. We've almost finished renovating the original groundkeeper's cottage for us to move into soon. Arvin's parents are so wonderful and his mum actually helps me find horses who are really needy. In fact, that's how I met Arvin. Through his mother. I just know you'll love her, Daphne. The way I do.' Belle picked up Arvin's hand and kissed his fingers. 'Meeting Heather changed my life so much for the better.'

'Mine too, babe.'

The love between the young couple was evident and reminded John of his early days with Daphne. They'd been married for several years by the ages of this couple, but he knew he'd looked at her the way Arvin was looking at Belle. Just maybe, he still did. Daphne was his love. They glanced at each for a moment and she smiled, the little laughter lines crinkling around her eyes. She was as happy as he was at finding Belle.

'Once we've had our coffee, shall we go for a walk around?' Arvin asked. 'And tonight we'll host a dinner for the wedding party, close family and of course, the two of you.'

Belle glanced at her watch. 'Actually, do you mind if I run inside for five minutes? I forgot to tell Susan, the head chef, the final numbers and with the restaurant so busy and me eating rather than working...' With a rueful smile she slipped from her chair. 'I'll catch up?' Not waiting for a response she hurried inside.

Daphne looked a bit confused. 'Eating rather than working?'

'There's so much you won't know. Belle is the sous-chef. Mum was head chef until Dad's accident and then Susan took over. Both of them have been wonderful mentors for Belle.'

'A sous-chef so young,' John said.

'She went into an apprenticeship after year nine at school. No interest in doing anything other than cooking and collecting horses. Now, may I show you around?'

. . .

'Are you certain I'm dressed up enough, love?' The one downside with Bluebell was the lack of big mirrors. There was only the small one in the bathroom and another inside the wardrobe door. That one was full length but very narrow and she could never quite manage to see all of herself in it at once.

John poked his head through the doorway and gave her the once-over.

'I didn't know you'd packed that dress but it looks perfect to me. Always loved the colour on you and I reckon it looks great with those shoes.'

You are such a good man.

The dress was three-quarter length in a classic cut and such a pretty shade of blue. Her shoes had higher heels than she usually chose and were black with silver buckles which matched her silver necklace and bracelets. With a black handbag and lightweight shawl, she hoped she'd made it come together nicely.

'And don't you look handsome.'

John always cut a fine figure in a suit and he wore his favourite dark blue pinstripe with a splash of colour by way of a blue and silver tie.

'We couldn't have coordinated any better, doll.' He held his hand out. 'All ready to head off?'

Once in the car, Daphne almost wanted to bounce up and down in her seat. Her earlier melancholy was gone and she couldn't wait to see Belle again. John carefully drove away from Bluebell and across to the main road and in a few minutes they were out of the town.

'Can you believe our Annabelle is living her dreams?' Daphne couldn't stop smiling.

'I'm very proud of her. So is Arvin. When you went after her, all he could talk about was how hard she's worked to get where she is and how compassionate and kind she is to anyone she meets.'

She hasn't changed a bit.

'The only thing which has me a little worried—' John slowed to turn into a narrower road. 'Not really worried. Just...'

'Do you mean Russell?'

He nodded.

'Hmm. Me too, love. He seemed decent the one time we met him before Annabelle left but if he had any part in discouraging her from talking to us, well, that does bother me.'

It more than bothered her. How hard would it have been to touch base now and then?

'We aren't here for him, though,' John said. 'Belle's an adult so quite able to make her own choices.'

'On a happier note, isn't the winery lovely?'

For the rest of the drive they chatted about their tour of the grounds earlier in the day. The massive barrel hall where all the different wines rested and turned into saleable product in their own time. They'd had a quick look inside the cellar door – the gorgeous tasting room which had a stone floor, stunning timber counter, and a wall filled with awards as well as boards detailing the history of the property.

'Did I hear right that Arvin's father is a drawcard for visitors with his lifelong knowledge of wines? He runs the cellar door now, rather than continuing as head winemaker.'

'Yes, Arvin is incredibly proud of his dad,' John said.

Before they'd seen where the ceremony was being held, Belle was needed back in the kitchen so new arrangements were made to meet the next afternoon. It gave Daphne a little more time to put the finishing touches to the ceremony and although she wished they'd had time to look at the area set aside for the wedding, she understood how Belle felt pulled in multiple directions.

'Goodness, look at how full the carpark is!'

It was almost at capacity but John found a spot at the very far end and it was only when they reached the top of the steps that Daphne suddenly grabbed his arm. What if Russell was hostile? Or their presence wasn't welcome tonight because they were – after all – only the celebrant and spouse.

John put an arm around Daphne and gazed into her eyes. 'We're here for the happy couple, doll. Nobody else. You look a treat and with your kind heart and wise words you'll win everyone over.'

She wasn't so sure but she trusted her husband and he had a way of making her see herself in a better light than her default tendency to downplay herself. Well, now was not the time for doubts.

FIVE

Daphne and John were welcomed by a charming maître d' who introduced himself as Kenny and ushered them to seats on one side of a rectangular table. There was a name on each place setting and they were first to arrive. Daphne's heart sank a little noticing Russell's name directly across from her but she smiled at John as he held her chair out. Might as well face Belle's dad immediately and get past any discomfort before the wedding.

'So Arvin's mother is next to me, on the end here, with her husband beside her.' Daphne was good at reading upside-down print. 'Russell's there. Someone called Lainie. Then a Brent, and that's as far as I can see.'

John peered at the name next to Brent. 'Owen. Then Arvin and Belle at that end. Rhianna and the final person, who is next to me, is Marsha.'

'Ah, now according to Arvin's information during our booking conversations, Owen is the best man with Brent as groomsman. Rhianna is matron of honour but I have a Tori as bridesmaid. And I wonder where Lainie fits in to all of this.'

'She's Russell's wife-to-be. According to her, anyway.'

Daphne jumped at the voice behind her but when she turned it was to look into the warm and amused eyes of an older version of Arvin. He was in a wheelchair and as he positioned himself at his designated place, she noticed for the first time there wasn't a seat there. She recognised him from the newspaper article.

'And you must be Daphne and John Jones,' he continued. 'Welcome to Crystal Springs. I hope my son didn't upset you too much with his novel approach to reconnecting you with Belle?'

'Novel is the word for it! But we are both so happy he made this happen,' John said. He got to his feet and walked around to shake hands with Eddie Kingsley. 'You have a gorgeous property.'

What did you mean by Russell's wife-to-be... according to Lainie?

People interested Daphne on a deep level. She'd always observed human nature and was a fair judge of character, despite occasionally trusting a little too quickly. Before she could ask anything, the table was suddenly inundated with guests finding their seats. Only Belle was missing. Arvin went around the table to each person with a quick hello, stopping to pull out the seat next to Eddie for a sweet-faced woman as she joined them.

'Dad, Mum? Please meet our celebrant, Daphne Jones. And her husband John. I think you know their connection to our Belle.'

'Your father's been making friends with them already, Arvin, now go find your bride and get her out of the kitchen.' Heather smiled at her son and when he obeyed, she reached a hand to Daphne's and squeezed. 'I'm Heather and I've been in on the secret for the last couple of weeks and cannot tell you how happy I am to meet you both. Belle is like a daughter.'

Such an easy woman to warm to. There was genuine kindness in Heather's face and Eddie was just as nice.

'Belle is fretting about the kitchen managing without her, so I'm expecting she'll run back and forth a bit.'

John leaned closer. 'We're so proud she's followed her dream of cooking professionally; I believe you were her first mentor?'

Eddie nodded. 'Heather saw her talent right away. Belle was only here for a month in a placement as part of her culinary course, but the minute she graduated she was knocking on the door for a job.'

'And I held it wide open.'

You truly are loved, darling girl.

Arvin returned alone. He stood behind his seat until everyone stopped talking and looked his way.

'Apparently the kitchen is short of a line cook so Belle is helping for a minute or two.'

'Oh darn. How strange.' Heather seemed to be speaking to herself, so quiet were her words. 'Everyone knows tonight is important.'

'While we wait, let's go around the table with introductions.' Arvin's eyes were on his father. And Eddie looked as puzzled as Heather.

'But we all know each other.'

The speaker was the woman seated opposite John. In her forties, she wore a white off-the-shoulder dress which accentuated her... well, chest, and a chunky necklace made of red beads. Her hair was cut into a pixie style and her skin was deeply tanned. On closer inspection, it appeared weathered from too much time in the sun. Despite her seemingly innocent comment, the woman had a smirk on her lips and ice-cold eyes which stared at Daphne.

The hairs stood up on Daphne's neck. Something was off.

'I'm sorry, I hadn't realised you already know John and Daphne.' Heather's tone was flat. No emotion.

'Apart from them, I meant.'

Heather came across as a person who liked everyone but her set expression said otherwise in this instance. Eddie slightly shook his head and took over from his son.

'Why don't we start with Daphne and John Jones then? Daphne will officiate the wedding we've all been waiting for. Do you both remember Belle's dad, Russell Boyd?'

Here we go.

Summoning a smile, Daphne finally looked across the table and almost wished she hadn't. Despite more than a decade since their one, brief meeting, his face was etched in her mind. A good-looking face which was currently flushed with colour. On his temple, a nerve twitched and that, oddly, settled her feelings a little. He was probably as worried about their reaction as she was about his. Mind you, he was the one who'd made bad decisions about keeping in touch. He was the one who'd taken Annabelle away when they'd wanted to adopt her. The same person who'd never been in the little girl's life until the moment he would have lost his parental rights.

John's hand found hers beneath the table as he spoke. 'Russell. Nice to see you.' His fingers tightened with his polite words and Daphne's resolve to stay in control almost crumbled. Only her husband's calm voice and warm hand stopped her speaking her mind.

'Wondered why the celebrant was invited to dinner. Only found out you were here about two hours ago,' Russell said.

It sounded like an accusation.

'We only discovered this was Belle's wedding late this morning. Imagine our surprise and delight to see her again after so long,' Daphne replied.

Russell narrowed his eyes but kept his mouth shut.

'Moving along,' Eddie said, 'Lainie Newman is Russell's friend—'

'Friend? Oh, Eddie. Friend is hardly the right description for our relationship.' The woman leaned toward Russell, who suddenly busied himself pouring water into a glass from one of several bottles which a waiter was placing around the table.

What did Belle say to me earlier? Russell and his friends? Did she mean Lainie?

'Then here we've got Brent and Owen, both long-time mates of Arvin as well as good all-round humans. Both play cricket with him each summer, taking him away from important work here.' Eddie grinned at the two young men, who gave him a thumbs up in unison. 'Next is Rhianna who is Belle's best friend and matron-of-honour.'

Rhianna was Belle's age, a slender woman other than her pregnant tummy, upon which she protectively rested one hand. Again, she'd been in the newspaper photo. She waved to Daphne and John with her other hand and they waved back.

'And Marsha, who has stepped in for Tori at the last minute.' Eddie picked up a glass of red wine with an almost dismissive air. 'To our bridal party... and the bride, who apparently loves us so much she is cooking our meal tonight!'

There was a resounding response of 'cheers' and some laughter but not everyone was amused.

By now, Daphne was immersed in people-watching and noticing small 'tells' that some were less happy to be here – or less happy with other guests here – than one would expect on a special evening. For example, Marsha and Lainie were sharing a long look... not hostile. More familial. The bridesmaid was younger than Belle and Rhianna and the closer Daphne looked, the more it was clear she was related to Lainie.

Well, well. And what happened to Tori?

The long gaze between the two included some rolling of their eyes and pouting. Very peculiar.

'Sorry, everyone! I'm here now.'

Belle wore an apron over her dress and carried a large tray filled with plates. Behind her were two servers with similar trays and all three began looking after the table. Arvin jumped to his feet and took the tray, first leaning across it to kiss the tip of her nose, which made her giggle.

John put an arm around Daphne and whispered, 'This is true love.'

She turned her face and smiled at him. 'It is. Just like us.'

When he pulled her close and kissed the end of *her* nose, she almost teared up. If Belle and Arvin enjoyed their future marriage even a tenth as much as she and John... well, they were in for a treat.

'But darling, the kitchen can manage even if down by one,' Heather said.

Belle moved around the table and leaned between Heather and Eddie, speaking just for them. But Daphne's sharp ears heard.

'Normally, yes. But Susan found out an hour ago that Godfrey Goffin has booked a party of four and we're worried they are all critics.'

'Oh no.' Eddie dropped his head. 'Not again.'

Had she heard correctly? *Not again?* What did Eddie mean and who was Godfrey Goffin that his name caused such a reaction?

Daphne didn't know who to ask.

Belle had moved to her own seat at last and everyone else was talking as meals were placed in front of them. Even John was chatting with the two young men across the table.

Heather had her hand on Eddie's shoulder and was whispering to him. He nodded a couple of times and finally straightened. Perhaps this Godfrey man was a rival or past friend. Except Belle had mentioned critics.

Food critics? Here to review the restaurant?

That would explain Belle's attendance in the kitchen. Short-staffed and potentially four food critics here all at once? Enough to unsettle the most prepared chef.

Daphne finally noticed a plate in front of her and her stomach rumbled. At least nobody would hear it over the talk at the table and background music but eating might stop it reoccurring at a more inconvenient time.

Served with the entrée was a delectable dry white wine from a bottle with the winery's label. Trying not to appear obvious,

Daphne attempted to read the description from a bottle with its back facing her, but the print was too small.

'We're proud of this one, Daphne,' Eddie said. 'Completely Arvin's doing, and although it could use another year in the cellar, I think you'll agree it already makes for easy drinking.'

'Very nice. John and I enjoy wine and try to take a few bottles home from the areas we visit.'

Heather smiled. 'We have every intention of making sure you have a lovely collection from here to take. At the wedding reception we're serving our gold medal-winning buttery Chardonnay to celebrate the day. And because we don't make sparkling wine here, our friends who have a winery in the Macedon Ranges have gifted us enough of their beautiful one to toast Arvin and Belle, and enjoy before and during the reception.'

By now John was listening to the conversation. 'Wonderful to be such good friends with other wine-growers and makers.'

'For the most part – certainly in this region – we all get on extremely well. Some of us share seasonal workers and send customers to one another.' Eddie frowned. 'Not all though.'

'Oh dear. Here we go.'

Heather's head had turned as three men and a woman followed a server to a table within easy sight, and possibly earshot, of the wedding group.

'I guess it could be worse,' Heather said. 'Godfrey is the only food critic. Those are his friends Jeremy and Warren Karlson and Jeremy's wife, Aleesha.'

'Try to ignore them, darling. As much as news of his impending arrival threw me, I know he thrives on being the centre of attention so let's not give it to him.' Eddie topped Heather's glass up, although she'd barely taken a sip. 'Let's drink to our new friends, Daphne and John.'

Holding the wine glass to her lips, Daphne waited until Heather lifted her own before drinking. All she wanted was to ask why the two of them were so stirred up about that man, but would it sound rude to do so? She already felt like she had new, lifelong friends in the couple and knowing they were upset on such an important evening was tugging at her heart.

Heather took a long drink then put the glass down a little too hard. Letting out a brief 'huff' sound, she looked at Daphne. 'You must wonder what on earth is going on.'

'I'm sure they don't want to know,' Eddie said.

I'm sure I do.

'Godfrey Goffin fancies himself as a celebrity food critic, Daphne. Of course that isn't his day job but in the past couple of years he's decided he is an expert and even has a snarky blog he publishes his reviews on.' Heather shifted in her chair to look directly at Daphne. 'Food critics are an important, if sometimes stressful, part of hospitality. They are usually fair and thorough though, so the onus is on the venue to deliver consistently high quality meals and service. But with Godfrey... well, he takes delight in tripping up staff and creating situations which some-times put a restaurant in an unfavourable light.'

For such a sweet and softly spoken woman, the bitterness in the last few words revealed how much this man had hurt Heather. And her family.

Daphne gently squeezed her arm. 'Well, he doesn't sound very nice. But if your head chef knows he's here, she'll be ready for anything. And I imagine your lovely servers are the same.'

'True. Susan is a warrior chef. She protects everyone in that kitchen and is incredibly talented. If anything, she's likely to go to his table and demand an apology if he tries anything.'

Eddie threw back his head and laughed, causing everyone at the table to look his way.

And everyone at Godfrey Goffin's.

Although their interest quickly returned to each other, one man kept his eyes on Heather and Eddie... and then moved them to rest on Daphne.

A prickle of unease made her smile at him. A forced, overly friendly smile which was her way of masking the uncomfortable feeling his scrutiny caused.

His face was stern, with heavy jowls reminiscent of a bulldog accentuating a frown. Someone spoke to him and after bizarrely winking at Daphne, he broke eye contact. It was an odd moment and left her in no doubt this was the food critic himself. She wasn't one to judge so quickly but something told her this wasn't a man to be on the wrong side of. At least she and John would never have to deal with him.

Dessert was finished and coffee coming out when Lainie picked up her phone and slung her handbag over a shoulder. 'No coffee for me, thanks, but I need a smoke. Marsha, you coming?'

'Mum, I told you I quit. So should you.'

With a shrug, Lainie tottered away on ridiculously high stilettos.

The evening had been enjoyable, with lots of laughter and talk. Belle had only just gone to see how the kitchen was doing after staying in her seat for the dinner. Around them, the restaurant was almost empty, with only the table of four and another with a couple remaining.

Arvin suddenly hurried to his parents, squatting between them and showing them something on his phone.

'I think we should ask him to leave, Dad.' Arvin's voice reached Daphne. 'And his party.'

Eddie's head was shaking again. 'There'll be hell to pay if we do.'

'Then how do we protect ourselves? Protect Susan and Belle and the staff?'

Heather took the phone and showed Daphne and John. It was a social media post with an image of a meal beneath the headline:

Another disappointment from Pinnacle.

And below the image – which was a bowl of plain pasta looking undercooked and no sauce – a paragraph.

After the debacle last year when I was served soggy vegetables and undercooked risotto, I was talked into giving this eatery a second chance. Let me just say that there won't be a third attempt. Good luck to anyone unfortunate enough to be fooled into thinking the quality of the food lives up to the pleasant surroundings. Time for yet another change of kitchen staff, if you ask me. And you should ask me, GG.

'Is this from that man over there? Godfrey?' Daphne was horrified. 'He's posted that while he's still here?'

Arvin nodded. 'That's his blog and it shares to several social media pages.'

For the first time Russell showed interest in what was happening this end of the table to look at the screen. Then he gazed at Eddie. 'This is nonsense. He's just trying to upset you.'

'Not even *our* food. Not *our* plate nor *our* table.' Arvin retrieved his phone and enlarged the image to prove his point. 'He's fabricating this.'

'Why, though?' Daphne asked. 'What does he have to gain?'

Eddie and Heather shared a quick glance.

Godfrey Goffin smirked at them from his table, going as far as to raise a glass as though toasting them.

Arvin straightened and Heather's hand grabbed his. 'Leave him, sweetie.'

The door to the kitchen flew open and a woman in chef's whites and hat stalked out.

'Uh-oh.' Eddie backed his wheelchair from his spot. 'How did Susan find out?'

Belle emerged from the same door and gestured frantically for Arvin, before following the other woman.

'The nerve of you, Godfrey!'

Susan wasn't yelling but her voice carried, getting the attention of everyone in the restaurant. The other couple stared, and Kenny stopped clearing a table and stood with his hands clenched together and mouth open.

'Don't be so melodramatic.' Godfrey was grinning ear to ear. 'Nothing a few more years in culinary school won't fix.'

Eddie weaved between tables and Heather followed.

'Do you think we should do something?' Daphne whispered to John. She had no idea what that something was.

'Take down that ridiculous review or I'll—'

'You'll what?' Godfrey got to his feet. 'Throw a tea towel at me? Or a knife?'

'Don't tempt me.'

'Would hardly be the first time.'

'This time I won't miss.'

'Okay, that's enough.' Eddie gestured to the front door. 'Time to go. Restaurant is closing now.'

The woman from Godfrey's party was on her feet in seconds and heading out with an outraged look on her face after saying she'd meet the others at the car. Only one of the men was still at the table and he observed with a small smile on an otherwise stern face.

'You won't be charging my table, of course.' Godfrey took his time putting on his suit jacket. 'I'll think about whether I send my review to the food magazines.'

Arvin got close to Godfrey, staring him straight in the eyes. For such a young man he had poise and courage. 'You will pay for your meal. You will take down that rubbish review. And you will publicly apologise for using a fake image to cause harm to our staff and family. Understood?'

Belle looked ready to cry and Daphne found herself out of her chair and hurrying to her before she realised what she was doing. But Susan had also noticed the younger woman's distress and put an arm around her shoulders. Godfrey and Arvin were staring each other down while Eddie and Heather backed off a little, probably hoping the heat would settle and sense prevail.

'You need to watch your back, fledgling. You think you're a real winemaker but would happily put a good one out of a career.' Godfrey directed this to Arvin then sneered at everyone else.

'Bunch of losers. Sue me for the meals. And expect a rapid loss of business once I share more insights. Night night.'

After Godfrey stalked out, brushing aside poor Kenny who'd tried to get payment, the feeling of celebration went with him.

'I think I left a pan on.' Susan almost ran back to the kitchen.

The other man at the table finally stood. 'I never know whether Godfrey is serious or just trying to amuse himself.' He collected his jacket. 'I'll pay for tonight.'

'Well, amusing himself is wrong when it affects peoples' livelihoods, Jeremy. Kenny will take care of you.' Heather glanced at the front desk where the other couple stood waiting. 'Oh, he must have gone to the kitchen. I'll take care of things.'

Heather took a couple of minutes to fix up the bills for the couple and the man called Jeremy. The whole time, Arvin's hands were clenching and unclenching.

'I'm going to make sure Godfrey is gone.'

'I'll come as well. Let's check he finds his way to his car.'

The rest of the party returned to the table and Russell got up to give Belle a hug. They spoke for a moment, which was the most Daphne had seen them interacting.

John busied himself filling glasses with what was left of the wine and handing them out. He'd only had one glass much earlier in the night and kept to water since, as he was driving. Everyone was quiet. Shocked. Belle had tears in her eyes and brought her chair around to Daphne's, leaning against her.

You poor darling. This isn't how a wedding week should be.

The moments dragged and Belle straightened. 'I should check where they are.'

Heather was sending a message. 'Just asked both Arvin and Eddie that same... oh, here they come.'

Arvin closed the door after his father wheeled through, turning a lock. Servers were clearing the last of the tables. Rhianna got a text and announced her husband had arrived and was meeting her at the top of the ramp. Belle went with her to the door to let her out. As she opened it, Aleesha Karlson peered in.

'Isn't he here?'

A chill went up Daphne's spine.

'We've all been waiting at the car so where is he? Where is Godfrey Goffin?'

John knew this feeling. He wished he didn't but the past year or so on the road with Daphne had taught him that criminals lurked everywhere. And sometimes they dragged his wife – and him – into helping solve mysteries.

She had a genuine knack for getting to the truth.

He was just there to support her.

And right now, there was an all-too-familiar expression on his wife's face.

She was listening to her gut and her gut was generally right. Whatever was happening tonight was not good.

'I asked where he is.' The woman pushed her way inside and stared around. When he didn't magically appear, she spun back to Arvin. 'What did you do?'

'Me? Dad and I followed him—'

'You've hurt him?'

'Of course not! We couldn't see him so came back.'

'He isn't just somewhere in the carpark?' John asked.

'There are fewer than ten cars there,' the woman snapped at him. 'Not that easy to miss a man his size.'

Belle had come back in from walking Rhianna to meet her husband. 'Well we didn't see him so perhaps he took a different path.'

Glancing around, John noticed the servers had all left the main room. Probably there was a big discussion going on in the kitchen between them, the cooks, Kenny and Susan. What a dreadful thing for a professional food critic to do. A bad review was one thing but fabricating a meal for the sole purpose of damaging the restaurant's reputation was a whole other level.

By now nobody was seated at their table. The two young men were either side of Arvin, while Russell, Lainie and Marsha stood a short distance away, the latter two both checking their phones.

'I wonder what he said to Kenny? As he left?' Heather asked.

Eddie looked around. 'Where is Kenny?'

'Who cares? I want a search party mounted right now and the police called. In fact I'll find my own police officer.' With that strange comment Aleesha stalked outside and disappeared along the path to the steps.

'Should someone go with her? Make sure she makes it safely to her car?' Daphne asked. 'John and I could do that.' She grabbed him by the arm. 'Just to the carpark and back, love?'

Knowing he had no say in the matter, John let her lead him outside and the minute the door closed, her energy lifted.

'Okay, doll?'

'I am but I fear Mr Goffin may not be.'

Just as he'd suspected. Her special senses believed foul play was involved in the events of the evening... particularly the last twenty minutes or so.

Here we go again.

For the first time tonight, Daphne regretted her choice of footwear, particularly as it had been raining earlier while they'd eaten and the ground looked slippery in parts. Her real prefer-ence was comfortable sneakers, followed by low-heeled smart shoes to match her wedding suits. But these pretty shoes matching her pretty dress had a two-inch heel and that might not work to her advantage should speed be needed. Or climbing. Or...

Good grief, Daph. What exactly do you think has happened?

There was no sign of the woman who'd left just before them, but a car door slammed in the distance.

'Slow down a bit. There's a good chance the man simply stopped to gather himself. Or went for a walk to calm down. Or decided to bypass his friends and go home on foot.' John was hurrying to keep pace.

'Do you know where he lives?'

'No. Do you?'

'Nope. But we are quite a way out from Benalla so unless he lives along the road back, it will be a long walk, don't you think?'

At the top of the steps, Daphne stopped, one hand up in a 'halt' position.

'Shall we go down?'

'Shh.'

She normally wouldn't shush her husband but there was a sound and she couldn't tell where it came from. And now it was gone.

'Did you hear that?' John was peering down the hill to the carpark.

'Like a moan?'

'Exactly like a moan.'

'Thought so; it came from over there.' Taking care of her footing, Daphne walked a bit beyond the path onto grass and pointed away from the carpark. 'I recall looking at that area when we drove in the first time and thought how steep and densely bushed it is.'

Another muffled sound came from the same direction.

Daphne pulled out her phone and turned on its flashlight. 'Would you run back to the restaurant and get Arvin or someone?' She started down the slope.

'Whoa, wait! We need proper lights and help.'

'That's what you are arranging, love.'

'Don't move. I mean it, Daphne.'

The alarm in John's voice stopped her and she looked back. He was worried.

'Stay here. Please, stay put and I'll be right back.'

'I'll wait.'

He was gone in a flash and she turned her light back to the slope. It didn't seem too bad here so she took a couple more steps but stopped as the ground began to drop away. The light didn't go as far as the bottom but a thought occurred to her and she returned to the path. From here she hurried down the steps and rather than enter the carpark, found a narrow dirt track leading the way she'd heard the moan. If someone had fallen, time would be of the essence.

This was the opposite direction from where Belle had run yesterday and while the tree she'd climbed into was in something of a parklike setting, over here was markedly different.

There was a sign.

NO ENTRY.

PLEASE RETURN TO THE CARPARK AND FOLLOW SIGNS TO THE

RESTAURANT OR THE CELLAR DOOR.

Each side of the track was filled with native shrubs, many overgrown. Being uneven and muddy it wasn't the easiest to walk along but then another moan spurred her on.

'Mr Goffin? Are you hurt?'

There was no response and she waved the light around hoping to find him. To her horror, something dark and wet pooled on the ground a few metres away and it wasn't from the earlier rain. She watched her step so as not to get too close and that's when she saw it.

A shoe. A shoe with a foot inside.

'Dandelions and daffodils,' she muttered as she dialled John.

'We're on our way, doll.'

'Maybe call an ambulance and come down the steps and go the

opposite way from the carpark. Past the NO ENTRY sign. And hurry.'

'Did you say ambulance?'

The foot moved and Daphne picked her way along the side of the track, her dress snagging on a shrub. She shoved her phone into a pocket to free herself.

'Mr Goffin? Help is coming.'

A whisper came in return… too faint to make out the words. Once freed from the bush Daphne shone her light on the foot, then up a leg and to a body which was face down, arms outstretched. Godfrey was on the other side of the track and barely moving. Too many crime scenes from the past made her hesitate. She could very well contaminate the area. But what if he'd simply fallen and needed help? Leaving the poor man there alone wasn't an option.

Daphne jumped across the track, grabbing the branch from a tree to steady herself as one foot landed in a soggy rut. She leaned down as close to the man's head as she could.

'My name is Daphne, Daphne Jones. There's an ambulance coming. Where are you injured? There was some blood on the path.'

One of his arms moved, the hand making an attempt to reach up to her. Daphne got onto her knees and took his hand. With surprising strength, he pulled her closer. His face – in the shadows cast by the light on her phone – was deathly pale. As much as she could tell, anyway.

'Tell… Susan.'

'Susan? Tell her what?'

'Knife…'

And with that, his hand dropped.

'Godfrey? Oh, dear.'

His eyes were vacant. She checked his pulse and there was none. There was no chance she had the strength to turn him onto his back to attempt CPR. That was when she noticed a narrow wound in the side of his neck. And a roundish-shaped one across the back of his head. How he'd even talked to her was a miracle.

'You poor man,' she whispered.

Her gut was screaming at her to do something but it was too late to save his life.

Can I find your killer?

It was wrong. Wrong on every level and might land her in hot water. Daphne opened her camera and began taking photos. She already was longing for her notepad and a pen, a quiet spot in Bluebell to sit and a nice cup of tea. That was how she'd solved several crimes in the past and while it might be antiquated and hardly glamorous... it worked for her.

Assuming a crime had been committed.

'Daphne?' John shouted from some distance.

She scrambled to her feet and turned the flashlight onto the wet patch on the track. 'Be careful. It looks like blood. He's over here and not in a good way.'

Not in a good way was an understatement. He might not have been a pleasant man but something terrible had happened tonight and she was going to get to the bottom of it.

The rain began again as Kenny performed CPR after he and two others had carefully turned Godfrey over. John led Daphne gently away and they stood beneath a tree on the other side of the path to let people through.

Daphne was close to John, quiet and with blood on her hands which she'd tried to clean off with some tissues. The skirt of her dress was ripped and she had barely said two words since warning everyone to avoid the pool of what looked suspiciously like blood in the middle of the dirt track. A pool which was being diluted by slow, large raindrops.

It was hard to believe this was how such a nice evening had ended.

Worse for him.

The wail of a siren drew closer and Kenny sat back on his heels, tears pouring down his cheeks. He'd tried to do the impossible. One look at Godfrey's face had made it clear to John the man was no longer of this earth.

Aleesha was sobbing, being comforted by one of the other men from their table: Warren.

'Everyone needs to move from the area.'

A voice boomed from behind John and he turned.

Jeremy was stomping down the middle of the track, pulling out his phone as he walked.

'Careful! There's blood. A potential crime scene.' Daphne waved and pointed.

'I'm a police officer.'

Nevertheless he did avoid the spot and went to check Godfrey, almost pushing Kenny out of the way. All he did was feel for a pulse in the man's neck and then straighten. 'Kenny, go to the carpark and meet the ambulance. Everyone else return to the restaurant and stay there until I come to question you. Warren, please make sure they do.' Jeremy tapped on his phone then glanced up. 'Go. All of you get out of the rain. Why do you have blood on you?' He suddenly crossed the path to Daphne.

'I found him. He reached for my hand. There's a cut on his neck.'

The police officer took another look at the body and shook his head. 'No, just one on his skull. Probably hit a rock falling. You're seeing things.'

Daphne was shaking and John wasn't allowing this man, even if he was law enforcement, to upset her further.

'We'll be in the restaurant, officer,' John said.

'I haven't finished speaking to her.'

'Come on, doll. Let's get you some tea.'

The other people followed and a glance over John's shoulder was met with a glower from the officer, who hadn't moved.

EIGHT

A towel around her shoulders, hands finally clean and wrapped around a hot cup of tea, the shaking slowly stopped. It wasn't from cold, but the adrenaline drop. Daphne had experienced this more than once after a traumatic experience and knew only time would settle her nerves.

Some answers might help.

Over and over her mind replayed the second she'd seen Godfrey's shoe. How long might it have been until someone found him had she and John not heard the moans? How did he get there? Was it possible he'd lost his footing and fallen, hitting his neck and head on the descent? Had there even been a cut on his neck? It was getting a bit hard to focus on the details.

'Daph? Would you like a brandy? Eddie suggested it might help us all feel a little less... upset.'

'Yes but no. Maybe once we get back to Bluebell but I'd rather keep my thoughts straight. How long do you think before they let us leave?'

John settled on the seat beside her. 'So that you can begin writing up those thoughts?'

His eyes twinkled, and despite the situation, she smiled. He knew her so well.

'What if I find some paper and a pen?'

'I normally have at least one notepad but wanted to bring my cute little bag tonight. To go with my dress.' She lifted part of the skirt. 'Look what I did to it.' So many rips in the soft fabric. Too much damage to fix.

'You did nothing, my darling girl, other than try to help a dying man. A torn skirt is nothing compared to the comfort you gave.'

He'd been openly worried when he'd arrived on the scene. By then she was on her feet and holding her hands away from her body. Her phone had fallen to the ground and the flashlight pointing up showed how much blood was on her. He'd picked it up and guided her away. Then the other people came. A procession of people. Arvin. Belle – who'd gasped and run back along the track after saying she had to find her. Whoever 'her' was. Aleesha Karlson and almost immediately the other man. Kenny. Eventually the police officer.

Now they were all here in the restaurant.

'Any ideas?'

'He may have fallen.' Daphne let her eyes roam around the room. 'Did Kenny come back?'

John shook his head. 'Last seen going to meet the ambulance.'

'Actually... where are Russell and Lainie?'

Daphne got to her feet to see better and John joined her. They were at the original table, which was cleared apart from a few personal belongings like handbags and phones.

'Belle, Susan, Eddie, Heather, all over there and having a very serious discussion. Owen, Brent, Arvin and three of the waiting staff seem a bit overexcited at the big window on the right. Marsha is alone tapping on her phone. And looking bored. The other two from Godfrey's table.'

Aleesha had stopped crying and was now jabbing her finger at Warren. It all seemed quite bizarre but not knowing any of them, or anything about them, Daphne moved on.

'No Kenny. And no Russell or Lainie. Hmm.'

'Odd. They were here when we came back.'

'Were they?'

'Pretty sure, Daph.'

'Would you mind finding me some paper?'

'Happy to make notes on your phone while you dictate.'

That was something he'd done before. John was much quicker on a phone and Daphne almost handed hers over. But she couldn't. What if he saw?

I'm going to go to jail for taking photos.

'No. I mean, thank you but on reflection I might wait until I'm back in Bluebell.'

She tried to ignore John's raised eyebrows.

'Here comes Belle.'

'Aunt Daphie... I'm so sorry I ran off earlier but I had to tell Susan about him. About Godfrey.'

The three of them sat to talk.

Surely Belle hadn't become the kind of person who'd gloat about the death of the enemy of a friend?

'You won't know any of the backstory, I guess.' Belle checked that nobody else was close enough to hear the conversation. 'She was married to him.'

'To Godfrey?' John asked in surprise. 'Is that why he wrote such a nasty review?'

Belle's head shook. 'More likely he was trying to get her atten-tion. He never wanted the divorce but he has a wandering eye and she got tired of it. Susan is very private and I couldn't bear her finding out with the staff around. She needed a chance to gather herself.'

How could I ever have doubted you?

'So you ran all the way back and told her... what did you tell her?'

'That you'd found Godfrey along the bush track, face down and not moving. An ambulance was coming. But also that there was a lot of blood.' Belle's face crumpled and her eyes glistened. 'I wasn't on the path long but I saw that. And how upset the both of you were. But I couldn't tell her right away. She wasn't in the restaurant. Not in the kitchen or cool rooms.'

Daphne's ears pricked up.

'Where did you find her?'

'She was just outside. On her phone. I can't believe this has happened. Not with everything Eddie and Heather have gone through. And not so close...' Belle's words trailed away, her bottom lip quivering.

'Your wedding is still happening, darling,' Daphne said. 'Nobody will blame anyone for an accident.'

John gave her a look. She knew the one. They'd both experienced enough of life to understand how people might put their own spin on things. See wrongdoing where it didn't exist or good where it was vacant. It went both ways. Sadly, the old saying of 'kicking someone when they were down' sometimes applied as well. Mob mentality. And hopefully not the kind of behaviour one would expect from the locals in this sweet town and surrounds.

Still... Godfrey Goffin and his friends were set on spoiling the reputation of the family and their business.

The door of the restaurant abruptly opened and Jeremy Karlson stood in the doorway, unmoving until all eyes were on him. Then, he stepped inside, leaving the door ajar.

A cool breeze followed, ruffling the edges of some of the tablecloths.

'Dramatic, much,' Daphne muttered to John.

'I have to call Dad,' Belle said. 'Lainie was finding this all upsetting.'

Did you roll your eyes?

Daphne hadn't seen Belle interact with Russell's 'wife-to-be' much tonight. Nothing which gave her the feeling they were close. Or otherwise. There was so much to consider. The last two days had been quite extraordinary. Not quiet. Not straightforward. Not in any way the wedding run-up she'd expected.

'We have a problem.' Jeremy found a spot in the middle of the restaurant and stopped, crossing his arms.

A dead guest will do that every time.

She needed to keep herself together. Not fall back on her quirky humour which got her through bad times.

The man looked around, ending up with his eyes on Daphne.

'Tonight we've lost a friend.'

There was a sound from the table with Eddie, Heather and Susan but who'd made it was unclear. Maybe all three.

'For anyone who doesn't know me, I'm Senior Constable Jeremy Karlson. Godfrey was my friend. He was a renowned food critic and well regarded in his regular job as an attorney.'

'This isn't the time for a eulogy.' Eddie wheeled toward him. 'So, it's true? He's really gone?'

'Don't sound so hopeful. Everyone knows his death is in your best interests.'

There were gasps of shock from Heather and Belle. Susan's mouth was tightly shut and her colour was high but she said nothing as Eddie stopped a couple of metres from Jeremy.

'What rubbish. None of us wanted anything bad to happen to him, despite his recent poor behaviour. Are detectives coming? If we're to be here for a while then we'll arrange some coffee and tea.'

'No need for detectives. It's clear Godfrey lost his footing coming down that steep incline. Probably was texting and walking and not watching his step. You're all free to leave but please use the ramp at the far end of the building to get to your cars. Local police are heading here to tape the area off and a doctor is attending shortly to examine him and likely sign a death certificate.'

This didn't sound right. Accidental deaths were usually referred to the coroner's office. Even those which looked straightforward. Daphne narrowed her eyes.

'Why were you all here tonight, Jeremy? Did you come to support his nasty game?' Susan was on her feet. 'You and Aleesha and Warren. All out to help him stir trouble on such an important evening for the family?'

Heather got to her feet and put a hand on Susan's arm. 'It isn't worth it, honey. Let it go.'

'Best listen to your boss's advice before you say something you'll regret.'

'Is that a threat?'

The silence dragged.

Russell wandered in as though nothing untoward had occurred tonight, oblivious to the stand-off until Belle grabbed his arm and whispered something.

'It was a suggestion, Susan. Back off and let the police do their job, unless you have something to hide? Anything you'd like to tell us?'

All the colour drained from Susan's face and she flopped back into her chair.

'I thought not. Everyone, go home.'

With that, Jeremy joined his friends.

Although John got to his feet, Daphne sat for a minute, trying to absorb as much as she could from the room. Her eyes missed nothing... well, she hoped not. Short of taking a video, she only had her powers of observation and memory to rely upon. A lot wasn't adding up and if she was to keep her promise to a dying man, she needed her wits around her and as much information as she could glean.

NINE

Instead of brandy, John made a big pot of tea and opened a packet of chocolate biscuits. Despite the late hour, Daphne needed to write down her notes and his thoughtfulness earned him a kiss.

He grinned. 'What was that for?'

'Being you. The sweetest and kindest man on the planet. I'd expected you to go to bed but here you are looking after me.' She almost yawned. The word 'bed' was enough to make her long to sink onto theirs and push away the upsetting images in her head.

'As your chief sounding-board, I'm not about to leave you to unravel tonight's events alone.' John slid into the seat opposite. 'I'll pour while you write. And talk. If you want.'

I do. But I can't tell you everything. Not yet.

Taking photos of a potential crime scene was out of character for her. Macabre, really. Probably against the law. And if Godfrey's death was ruled an accident then she would delete them.

'But what if it wasn't?'

'Wasn't what?' John asked.

'Sorry, thinking aloud. An accident.' Daphne opened a new notebook. This one had a purple cover with a white rose in the corner. Pretty and practical with its mix of lined and unlined pages which would allow her to attempt rough sketches if she chose. 'I might start with all the names and what we know.'

With John's help she soon had a long list and a brief comment beside most names – such as their relationship to the restaurant and where they were when Godfrey left.

Looking over the notes, John pointed to Kenny's name. 'Did you see him speak to Godfrey as he left?'

'No. I got the feeling Godfrey brushed him off but I recall Heather saying something about it.'

'She wondered what Godfrey had said to him. Maybe she saw more than we did. And then Eddie asked where he was. Kenny.'

'I feel a lot of people had hurt feelings tonight. And poor Kenny tried so hard to resuscitate Godfrey when there was no life left in the man. Did you see the tears on his face?' Daphne reached for a biscuit. 'These are naughty, John Jones.'

'And delicious.'

After eating her biscuit and drinking some tea, Daphne started a new page. 'I know the death is supposedly an accident, but just in case... well, you know me, love.'

'What are you thinking?'

'While things are fresh in my mind I might jot down who we know for certain could have had nothing to do with the incident. Mainly because they were in our sight between the time he left and the time we heard him moaning.'

'Even from before then.'

Daphne tilted her head in question.

'By posting that review, Godfrey potentially put a metaphorical target on his back and—'

'Oh, you are clever. The killer may have left before he did.'

'Killer?'

She shrugged. 'Theoretical killer.'

'Yet Senior Constable Karlson declared this was an accident. Don't accidents need to be referred to the coroner?'

'You've spent too much time hanging around me, love. But yes, that's my understanding. And I would have thought he'd at least have spoken to me about my conversation with Godfrey before... you know.' His last words. 'Now that I'm here where I feel safe and loved, more is coming back. I need to write this down. He spoke to me.'

'He did?'

'Yes. Tell Susan.'

John's expression was almost comical in its confusion. She pushed the biscuits closer to him.

'Have another and I'll explain as I write. He grabbed my hand and said, "Tell Susan".'

'Susan? Tell her what?'

'That is exactly what I said! I mean, all I knew was she'd been terribly upset with his review and he'd seemed incredibly smug about it.'

'Did you get an answer from him?'

'The last thing I'd have expected. One word. "Knife".'

'Oh. No wonder you think there might be more to this. But even though Susan was upset, she doesn't seem the type to murder a guest. Even a bad one.'

'How about one who is her ex-husband. Who had given her cooking bad reviews before. And besides, we know all too well that sometimes the person one least expects turns out to be a dreadful human.'

They nodded at each other.

Some of the criminals Daphne had exposed didn't fit her idea of a killer. They came from all walks of life and a range of ages. Some were kind to everyone while others were more reclusive but respected in their community.

'Just for once it would be nice if a genuine bad guy was my chief suspect *and* the perp.'

The word made John laugh and then he collected their empty tea cups and got up to wash them.

Daphne flicked the page back to the one with the long list of names. Was someone there a killer? Or was Godfrey Goffin's death nothing more than a tragic accident?

. . .

John drove through the open gates of Crystal Springs with a sense of déjà vu. It was almost twenty-four hours since he'd parked the car to leave Daphne to do her job, only to have the joyful surprise of reuniting with Belle.

Today though they were here because Belle had phoned as they finished breakfast, asking them to come over. Daphne was still putting finishing touches to the ceremony but didn't hesitate to agree. If Belle needed them then they would rearrange any other plans. As they approached the carpark, police tape fluttered at the entrance to the narrow track. It was sobering.

There was a marked police car and a van with 'Crime Scene Unit' parked along with a handful of other vehicles but not a person in sight.

'Does this feel a bit like yesterday? But without the knowledge someone died here overnight?' Daphne was gazing in the direction she'd found Godfrey.

'It does. As upsetting as it all is, we're here for Belle and Arvin. I can't imagine how worried they must be about their wedding.'

'And the long-term damage to the restaurant. To the winery.'

They climbed out and looked around. All was quiet. Other than the official cars and police tape it might be an ordinary day with nothing out of the ordinary. John sighed. He didn't mean to but Daphne heard and reached for his hand to hold as they walked up the ramp.

'You're here!' Belle burst out of the front door of the restaurant and hugged Daphne and then John. 'I know this wasn't the schedule but... well, this is all so distressing. Arvin is down at the barrel hall. We can talk on the way.'

'Are you alright, dear? Last night was a big shock for everyone and we've been thinking about you all,' Daphne said.

'It *was* a big shock. Back this way.' Belle headed the way they'd come but rather than going down the ramp, continued along a path. 'Eddie is great. He's arranging a counsellor to come out soon and spend time with all the staff. Heather is very quiet which worries me but Arvin says she's just dealing with it in her own way. Susan has shut down.'

'How so?' Daphne asked.

'She was here until about two this morning, insisting on cleaning the kitchen from top to bottom and refusing any help. Down this set of steps is quickest.'

The steps took them away from the path, which went off in a different direction.

'Is it normal for the head chef to do most of the cleaning as well?' John asked. 'Seems a lot on top of all her other tasks.'

'Not normal but I kinda understand. She just lost her ex and their last words exchanged weren't at all friendly. Susan takes great pride in how she runs the kitchen and the quality of the menu and meals. She arrived about an hour ago and won't talk about anything other than the kitchen or the wedding.'

'At least the wedding gives everyone something good to look forward to,' Daphne said. 'And if you like we can go over my notes for the ceremony this morning while I'm here, instead of later.'

At the bottom of the steps they cut through a few dozen old trees. John figured this was where Daphne had followed Belle to talk yesterday. Ahead was the barrel hall, the tasting cellar and a carpark catering for them.

'Oh... sorry, Auntie. You probably needed a bit more time. I'm just worried.' Belle slowed and put her arm through Daphne's. 'We didn't really get a chance to look at where we are having the wedding and the hire company phoned and wanted a final plan and I don't know and some people have cancelled because of Godfrey and—'

'Annabelle. Sorry, Belle. Stop for a minute.' John held his arms out and she stepped into his hug. 'I'm sorry anyone has cancelled but your big day is going to be absolutely wonderful.'

'He's right, dear. There's always hiccups but anyone who matters will be there. And we'll help you finalise the setup. We're good at it. I can't wait to see your dress and the groom and your wonderful bridal party all dressed up.'

'Other than Marsha,' Belle muttered. She released John. 'Sorry. That's not charitable.'

'Not wanting to pry, but I thought your friend Tori was the bridesmaid?'

'Me too. But she came off her motorcycle last week and broke her ankle and her arm. A car hit her back wheel and she's lucky to be alive.' Belle's eyes filled with tears. 'I told her I don't care if she's being pushed in a wheelchair and even tried to make her laugh about potential races with Eddie at the reception; his suggestion. But she thinks she's let me down. Oh why is everything so complicated?'

'What a dreadful accident. So why Marsha?'

John wasn't at all sure he could be so to-the-point but Daphne had no qualms. She wanted to know what was going on in the background of the wedding. Get a broader perspective. Be prepared for anything.

'Dad asked. I think Lainie made him. Then when I said I wasn't sure what to do, she came around to the house with a huge box of expensive chocolates and told me it would be a kind gesture as Marsha feels left out. She's the same dress size as Tori so could easily step in. And while she's not a friend as such, it made Dad happy. I think.'

Raised voices interrupted the conversation. Two male raised voices. Coming from inside the barrel hall.

'Not more arguing. This is what I was afraid of.'

TEN

At least Daphne was wearing sensible shoes today and was able to keep up with John... although not Belle, who'd disappeared through the open doors and was nowhere to be seen. The raised voices had become a shouting match and that was never a good thing.

This was a large stone building with a stone floor and the temperature drop from outside was notable. Perfect for keeping barrels cool but a bit brisk compared to the pleasant morning sunshine. This was where much of the wine was stored as it matured and along one side was an area where the wine was made. Huge vats, a sorting bench, and all manner of instruments Daphne didn't recognise.

And two men, face to face, and furious.

Arvin and a much older, much shorter man who was waving his arms around in utter frustration. Both were yelling. Neither was listening. And Belle was trying to get between them.

'For the last time, Claude, I did *not* leave the door unlocked!' Arvin bellowed.

Putting two fingers between her lips, Daphne sucked in some air and hoped her old whistle would work. It did, echoing as everyone turned to look at where the shrill sound had come from.

She was quite impressed with herself. Back when she and John had foster children, she'd learned to do that for times they were on a windy beach or a sprawling park. Much better than raising her voice.

'You both need to stop this!' Belle's voice shook. 'Saturday is my wedding day and there's been more than enough upsets already without the two of you acting like children fighting in a sandpit.' She crossed her arms and each man took a couple of steps back.

'I'm sorry, sweetie.' Arvin drew in a long breath. 'Sorry, Claude.'

Claude was in his late fifties, bald, and had what Daphne would normally consider to be a kind face with lots of laughter lines. It was far from kind now as a scowl darkened his expression. The man seemed torn between continuing the argument and civil conventions and, thank goodness, the latter won.

He extended his hand to Daphne and spoke with a slight accent... French if she was not mistaken. 'Apologies. I am Claude Benoit, the head winemaker.' His eyes flicked toward Arvin when he'd said his title then back to Daphne. 'We mean nothing by our loud voices.'

'You know that's not true!'

'Belle, please—'

'No, Arvin. Why are you both at each other again? There's so much to do before tomorrow yet here you both are, squabbling and wasting time.'

Arvin's head dropped.

John shook Claude's hand. 'Nice to meet you. I'm John Jones and this is my wife Daphne, who is officiating the wedding.'

'I say good luck to that.'

'What do you mean, Mr Benoit?' Daphne asked ever so sweetly.

'Weddings are happy. People smiling and music and vows and lots of my wine. Not police and crime scenes and chaos. How can one celebrate with death lurking so close?'

Belle's hand flew to her mouth.

He gazed at her, his expression sad. 'You deserve a day all about you, Miss Belle.'

'Then why won't you help me? Nobody expected a tragedy last night but I'm still going to marry Arvin. Yet the two of you can't seem to agree on anything anymore!'

Uh-oh. That temper is still there beneath the surface.

'I remember you both working into the night to perfect a new mix. And you, Claude? Taking precious time from your own work to help Arvin when he was stuck with his first vintage. And after Eddie's accident you virtually saved the vines on your own. What changed? Tell me, what changed?'

A strange silence fell. Daphne felt she was holding her breath waiting for some response. Belle's words were a plea for understanding. For a better time.

Arvin's face was so sad.

Claude shook his head. 'Ask your father, Miss Belle.'

And with that enigmatic statement, he turned on his heel and stalked away.

I'm going to need to invest in running shoes which look like dress shoes at this rate.

Not that Daphne was running but she was walking briskly to stay close enough to Belle to listen in on her conversation with Russell. It might be wrong and nosy but quite necessary.

John and Arvin were behind her, going at a more reasonable pace and deep in quiet conversation. Knowing John, he was gently offering advice or support to the young man, who must be struggling with his own worries about the wedding, given the death of the food critic and the latest turn of events.

They were all heading toward the lake to look at the spot where the ceremony would take place. But almost the minute they'd left the barrel hall, Belle had whipped out her phone and muttered something about calling her father. And she'd sped away.

What exactly did Claude mean about Belle's wedding day?

He'd seemed sad. Hadn't Belle mentioned she thought the wine-maker was being courted by another winery? Could that be the reason he and Arvin were at odds? But what did it have to do with Russell? By now there was a fair gap between Daphne and the boys so when Belle suddenly stopped, then plonked onto a bench, she knew she had a minute or so to listen.

'Daddy, you have to be honest with me.'

Daphne came to a halt. She was within earshot but unnoticed.

'Claude said to ask you why things have changed between him and Arvin. What have you done?'

Whatever Russell's response was only reached Belle's ears. Pity she hadn't put the phone onto speaker.

This really is none of your business, Daph.

'What makes you think I know what Claude's going on about?'

Wait on... that was Russell's voice. Belle motioned for Daphne to join her at the bench, where she'd put her phone on speaker. Any embarrassment at being caught snooping vanished when Belle winked at her.

'What exactly did he say?' Russell asked.

'To ask you.'

There was an audible sigh from Russell. Frustrated, if Daphne wasn't mistaken.

'Why can't anything be simple, Belle? There's no conspiracy to stop your wedding, so stop fretting over nothing and concentrate on being a beautiful bride. Claude knows Arvin will be taking over from him sooner or later so for all you know, he expects it to be sooner. I know how proud you are of Arvin's talent for winemaking.'

'Yes I am. But, no, Dad. The arrangement is that when Claude wants to retire then Arvin will step up but that's ages away. At least a few more years.'

'Not really necessary though, is it? Waiting, I mean.'

Belle's eyes widened as they shot up to meet Daphne's. She mouthed 'this is weird' while Russell continued.

'Claude has done his bit for Crystal Springs and he's not

getting any younger. Probably hanging out to retire. Arvin's time to shine. Head winemaker and heir to the winery? You've done well for yourself, kid.'

Arvin and John had almost caught up and Daphne discreetly pointed to them so Belle was aware. She immediately tapped the phone to take it off speaker and put it to her ear.

'Nice chat, Dad. Talk later.' She ended the call and whispered to Daphne. 'Can we have a private talk? Soon?'

The setting for the wedding ceremony was simply lovely. John was itching to start taking photos. The lake itself wasn't huge but would easily accommodate a few rowboats. At one end was a rustic boathouse with a jetty and this was to be the backdrop of the wedding. Ducks and geese enjoyed the still water which reflected lazy clouds high above.

A ute with a trailer was parked nearby and two people wearing overalls unloaded potted flowers into the boathouse.

'We had the idea of using the flowers as a kind of border then chairs in a few rows,' Arvin said. 'There's about eighty people attending.'

'Closer to sixty now.' Belle held the screen of her phone in his direction. 'All the party from Wodonga have cancelled and that was twelve people in a minibus.'

'Why would they all cancel?' Daphne asked. 'Surely not because of last night?'

Belle shrugged.

'Then they'll be missing a beautiful event.' John put an arm around her shoulders. 'How are you arriving?'

'You'll think me silly.'

'It isn't silly, babe. On horseback,' Arvin said.

'Oh, I love that idea!' Daphne's face lit up. 'One of your rescues?'

'Yes. Tilly is her name and she's just a sweetheart. She's pure chestnut so matches my hair.' Belle laughed, running a hand through her long locks. 'Fortunately she's placid and not at all fazed by my dress and stuff.'

'Are your guests allowed to take photos?' Images were popping into John's mind of how to capture the perfect image of her. 'I know some wedding photographers are protective of their events.'

'We're encouraging it. The photographer will take all the official photos but we're hoping for lots of cameo and casual shots as well.' Arvin gestured to the lake. 'We're going to try to get some taken in a rowboat.'

'If I don't fall in.'

'I won't let you.' Arvin grinned at Belle. 'And there'll be plenty of people to help you in and out of the boat with your dress.'

She didn't look completely reassured but smiled at her fiancé.

Whatever were you and Daphne up to earlier?

He knew Belle had phoned her father but when he and Arvin caught up, she was sitting on a bench with Daphne having a quiet word. And then Daph had given him one of her looks... the kind which said there was information to share later.

For the next half hour he and Arvin helped the men with the flowers set up the border after roughly working out how many chairs and how much space needed for the podium and aisle. Belle and Daphne went for a walk around the lake. The ladies were almost back when the police car drove down from the carpark and pulled onto the grass. Two officers got out and wandered across to the lake and by the time they reached John, Daphne and Belle were back.

Arvin offered his hand. 'Hello, Joyce. And Perry. You know Belle?'

Both nodded.

'These are our friends and guests, Daphne Jones and John Jones.'

'Good morning. I'm Constable Woodcroft and this is Constable Freeman. We've finished up at the scene of the unfortunate incident and the crime scene van will shortly follow.'

There was an awkward silence. But John knew his wife too well and she didn't let him down.

'Nice to meet you both. May I ask... did you know... I found Mr Goffin. Before he passed away. Is there anything you need to speak with me about? Any questions?'

Constable Joyce Woodcroft shook her head. 'Our understanding is that Senior Constable Karlson took care of that already. Last night.'

'He didn't ask me anything. Well, that's not true. He asked why I had blood on my hands and arms. But nothing else.'

The constables exchanged a puzzled look.

'It's just that I've been involved with some crime scenes in the past and it seems odd nobody wants a statement.'

'Crime scenes?'

'Well... more that there's been a couple of sad deaths at previous events I've officiated. I was able to assist the police with finding the culprits.'

'Auntie?'

'Oh, it isn't anything to worry about, dear.' Daphne sent a flustered look in John's direction. 'And neither happened during the actual wedding ceremony.'

Belle's eyes were wide and Arvin didn't seem to know where to look. The police though had their attention on Daphne and if he didn't do something soon, there'd be all kinds of questions and speculation. Just for once, John wished Daphne had kept her thoughts to herself. Nobody was under suspicion. The police were just being polite. And until now, Belle and Arvin had no idea of the past cases Daphne had helped solve.

But Daphne gathered herself and raised her chin. 'If you don't mind, constables, I'd like to provide you with a statement. I didn't know Mr Goffin, but surely he deserves his final moments to be properly recorded?'

The officers stepped away to have a word and Daphne exhaled.

'Which people died at your ceremonies?' Belle asked.

'Um... er...'

'A bride?'

'No. No of course not.'

Belle looked slightly less worried. 'A groom?'

Oh dear me.

'Mrs Jones?' Constable Freeman interrupted.

Thank the stars.

'We'll have a chat with our senior officer and if she thinks it appropriate, we'll be in touch to arrange a statement.' Constable Freeman took out a notepad. 'May I take your contact details?'

'I'll give you my business card.' Daphne rummaged in her handbag before drawing one out. 'Phone is best. Or email.'

As soon as the police were back in their car, Belle grabbed Daphne's arm. 'We need to talk!'

ELEVEN

Daphne was certain she'd messed up by mentioning crime scenes and the like. She'd not thought it through, being more concerned about justice for the dead man than considering her past foster-daughter had no idea about the unfortunate deaths – murders – of a groom and a guest at different weddings. For the second time since arriving in Benalla, she expected Belle to ask for a different celebrant. And that made her heart heavy.

They were back in the restaurant, seated around a table for four against one of the long windows. Belle had gone to the kitchen to arrange coffee for them all, after saying little on the walk back despite her insistence they talk. None of them said much and for Daphne, that ramped up an old childhood anxiety she'd not felt in a while. It felt like waiting for an explosion to occur.

'Before Belle returns, is there anything I need to know?' Arvin hadn't looked at Daphne until now.

I've given you such a scare, poor love.

His face was drawn and rather than being able to worry about nothing more than his wedding, he had the weight of the world on him.

'Just that neither of you need to be stressing over what's happened before. We're here for your big day and nothing will stop that happening.' Hoping that would reassure him, Daphne plastered on a smile she didn't feel.

'I really didn't think this through,' he muttered more to himself than them. 'All I wanted was to fulfil Belle's dream of seeing you both again, but why didn't I do more research? It wasn't all that hard to find you once I knew your names and the town and then seeing you were a celebrant was like a sign. But this new information...' Arvin sighed heavily.

'Daphne has never done anything other than help people at the time they needed it the most.' John's tone was mild. 'Her presence as a celebrant had nothing to do with the evil intent of people she'd never met before the day, so before you judge her... or judge yourself... remember the love she wrapped around Belle as a lost and sad child. My wife has the biggest heart of anyone I know.'

Tears prickled at the back of Daphne's eyes and she rapidly blinked.

'Sorry, Daphne. I didn't mean to sound negative.'

She shook her head. 'Last night was hard for everyone.'

Belle approached with a tray and like he'd done last evening, Arvin jumped up and took it from her, holding it as she transferred steaming mugs of coffee and a plate of cupcakes to the table.

'There's a mix of flavours so do try them all.' Belle took her seat. 'Susan wants to know if you're coming for dinner tonight.'

But do you even want us here?

Her heart was beating a little too fast. How could she answer when she didn't know?

Then a warm hand took hers beneath the table and John spoke. 'Would you mind if we let you know once Daphne's had a chance to finish off the ceremony? There's not an exact science to timing when it comes to crafting the beautiful words she writes.'

He either had no idea how tenuous her position was as celebrant or was bluffing to cover his concern, but either way she loved him more at this moment than ever before. If only the churning in her stomach would go away. After all, the worst that could happen was Belle asking for a new celebrant. And sending her away. And never speaking to her again.

'Auntie? Oh, dear Aunt Daphie, why are you crying?'

'I'm not...' But her hand was wet when she touched her face.

Belle leaned closer, trying to put both arms around Daphne from too far away and almost losing her balance, which made them both laugh and broke the tension. Then Belle straightened and passed her a napkin.

'It must have been awful finding Godfrey like that. Being the person who was there when he took his final breath. No wonder you're emotional. Should I fetch some wine or something?'

The kindness and concern in Belle's voice almost brought a new rush of tears, but Daphne drew in a long breath and took off her glasses to dry her eyes.

'The coffee is fine, dear. And yes, it wasn't a pleasant experience but at least the poor man had me there at the end.'

Arvin pushed the cupcakes toward Daphne. 'Have some of these. They'll cheer you up, guaranteed. Belle made them.'

They did look and smell delightful. Each had a different icing and swirl of hearts or stars or...

'Are those horses?'

'Sure are.'

Daphne picked up a cupcake and peered at the icing. 'The detail is fantastic. I can see the eyes, and how pretty is that mane?'

Belle beamed. 'This is Tilly. If you like we can go down to the paddocks later and I'll introduce you.'

This didn't sound like someone who wanted to find another celebrant.

'Does this mean you want me to officiate the wedding... still?'

'Of course. Why would you think otherwise?'

The front door opened and Heather followed Eddie in. They didn't look around or notice the four people around the table as they headed straight for the kitchen. Nobody spoke until they'd gone in, the door flapping back and forth in their wake.

'Auntie, I wanted to talk to you because we need your help.

Until earlier... at the lake, I had no idea you had experience with solving stuff. Bad stuff. And I think we could do with your help.'

'Belle, maybe you shouldn't...' Arvin shuffled in his seat.

'I'll always help you, but how?'

Lowering her voice, Belle gazed at Daphne. 'It's about the letters.'

'The letters? Which letters?'

This was an interesting turn of events. Arvin didn't seem very pleased about it but Belle lifted his hand and kissed his fingers.

'I think we should tell them, babe.'

'But is it up to us?'

'Do you think your parents will ask for help? They didn't even want us to know.'

Ooh... colour me intrigued.

'Besides, Daphne is some kind of private detective so—'

'Sorry to interrupt, but I'm really not any kind of detective. I just have a nose for truth and a small talent for observing human behaviour.'

John made a snorting sound and everyone looked at him.

'Okay, so perhaps you don't have an official title, but you've been instrumental in finding more than one killer, as well as thieves and other criminals, which is why I call you a celebrant sleuth.'

Belle clapped her hands. 'Celebrant sleuth is perfect!'

Before the conversation became entirely derailed, Daphne picked up her cup. 'Tell me about these letters.' The coffee hit the spot, hot and delicious as she savoured several mouthfuls.

After a long look at his fiancée, Arvin spoke. 'I'll tell you about them but I don't see how this has anything to do with what happened last night. With Godfrey, that is. And it is best Dad and Mum don't know we're having this discussion.' He gazed around the table and everyone solemnly nodded. 'It all began a few months after Dad's accident, which was close to three years ago.'

On that enigmatic note, Arvin leaned toward the middle of the table and the rest of them followed suit. His voice dropped and a tingle of excitement scurried up Daphne's spine.

'Dad was the third generation winemaker at Crystal Springs and his entire world revolved around the perfect vintage, Mum and me, and being general manager of the vineyard and winery. Mum ran the restaurant and was head chef. He had specialists and assistants in each main area, including a dedicated bookkeeper and ground staff. One took over the day-to-day affairs during Dad's long recovery. His car was hit by a truck late one night and it was a miracle he survived.'

'What a dreadful time for you all,' John said.

'We thought the worst part was the crash and the hospital stay and then the recovery period. It was more than ten months before he was back here all the time. And weeks more until he felt up to looking at the reports, particularly the finances. It was a dreadful shock.'

Belle took over. 'Heather had hired Susan the minute she realised how much time she'd need to spend in Melbourne. Sometimes she was gone for a week at a time while Eddie was recovering. And Arvin was down there a lot as well. The support was part of what made Eddie fight so hard to survive, I'm certain of it.'

Arvin's head dropped and Belle leaned over and kissed his cheek.

The restaurant was completely empty other than their table. Perhaps there was a staff meeting in the kitchen. Although, wouldn't Belle be part of it?

'You said Eddie had a shock about the running of the property?' John prompted.

'Yes. While the restaurant was doing well, and the wine was still being crafted by Claude, there'd been a dramatic lowering of standards caring for the rest of the property. And the bookkeeper had syphoned a lot of money into their own account. There was a time when Dad said he'd sell up but Mum and I talked him out of it.'

'Oh, my,' Daphne breathed. 'What a dreadful blow. First a life-altering accident and then to find the people you trusted to run your business were destroying it. Did the bookkeeper repay the money?'

'Yes. Some, anyway. Because back then we had a lawyer who was clued up and ready to set right the damage done by a criminal to the place where his wife worked.'

His wife worked? Wait... a lawyer?

'Am I thinking about the same person?'

'Yes. Godfrey Goffin was the estate's lawyer and still married to Susan at the time. He was relentless in pursuing the funds and helped save us. Financially, anyway.'

An almost overwhelming amount of information was vying for attention in Daphne's brain. An accident. Embezzlement. Neglect of duties. A lawyer who was once an ally and became an enemy.

'The community gathered around us,' Arvin said. 'There were fundraisers held. Working bees including several other local wineries sending their own staff to help get the vines back on track. It was an incredible time for us seeing how much the winery meant to people in the region and how generous humans were. It made all the difference to Dad. His spirit rose and he and Mum were determined to make it work.'

'But then came the letters.' Belle's eyes were wide. 'Everything changed again.'

Arvin leaned even closer. 'It began with one.'

'Hello! How long have you all been there?' Heather's friendly voice cut through the moment of suspense. 'Are you working on the ceremony?'

Bother. I mean, I really like you but I also really need to know about these letters!

'Not too much to do now,' Daphne said with a big smile. 'We'll head off soon so I can tinker with the words but I feel we are on the same page.'

A page called a letter. Or several letters.

'But you'll stay for lunch? We open soon.'

'Susan's invited John and Daphne to come for dinner. But I'm sure they need some time together to explore our town.' This was Arvin, who got up and went to give his mother a kiss. 'I'm going to be a bit cheeky but would love to see your caravan... Bluebell?'

John beamed. 'Why don't you both come and visit us? We're on the little island camping site.'

'Can we?' Belle stood. 'I have to do lunch but we could drop by mid-afternoon if that suits?'

'Please do. By then I'll have the final words ready for you to look at and we can enjoy a nice cuppa in Bluebell.'

And finish our conversation about these mysterious letters.

TWELVE

While Daphne settled at the table with her notes and copy of the ceremony, John made cheese and tomato sandwiches for their lunch. There was so much to discuss before the youngsters arrived but first, his wife needed a little time to work without interruption. He quietly placed her plate on the table and took his own outside. Her head was down, pen in hand, but she'd whispered, 'Thanks, love.'

He wandered down near the water and sat on a bench he'd noticed earlier. The shade of a large gum tree took the bite out of the heat of the afternoon sun.

What a pretty place this is.

Travelling with Daphne was his new favourite thing to do after decades living in Rivers End. That would always be their home. Their safe haven. But there was a certain freedom being on the open road and Bluebell gave them the option of stopping almost anywhere camping was permitted. It had begun as Daphne's dream but was now his passion too.

If only we didn't keep stumbling across people who break the law.

As well as the unfortunate murders Daphne had helped solve, there'd been other crimes such as theft and perverting the course of justice and embezzlement. Which brought him back to the book-keeper who'd stolen from Crystal Springs when it was down... and the lawyer who'd recovered much of it. What a strange turn of events. Presumably the divorce of Godfrey and Susan had changed the man into someone who was vindictive and tried to damage the business he'd once helped save. There was no understanding some people.

The lake was full of ducks and geese and after finishing his sandwich, John took a series of photos. Hopefully things would settle down after the wedding and he could spend some time fishing. He'd not made any of Daphne's favourite dishes for a while – fish tacos and fish pie.

Across the strip of water was a carpark near the library. There was a solitary car parked close to the water and a man was leaning against it, smoking. Although he faced away from John, he was almost certain it was Jeremy, the police officer. And as he watched, a second car arrived, parking beside the first. The man turned around and John saw that it wasn't Jeremy, but his brother, Warren.

Goodness they look alike from a distance.

The driver's door of the second car opened and a woman in a short skirt and stilettos climbed out. *Lainie?*

Well, this was interesting. Wishing he was close enough to hear, something made him open his phone camera and start video-ing. Must be too much time spent with Daphne, who never missed the chance to collect clues.

How on earth is this a clue though? One of these people is Belle's father's girlfriend!

He stopped recording, feeling a bit ashamed of himself. These weren't clues. Neither Lainie nor Warren had done anything to be considered suspects in the unfortunate death last night. Warren had even helped after the event by fetching towels, and seemed a pleasant chap.

No, this was a meeting of the clandestine kind, if the long kiss on the other side of the water was anything to go by. Poor Russell.

But after a few minutes, the kissing turned to a conversation which became heated. John starting recording again, pushing away the nagging voice of reason. Easy enough to delete it later.

John had been gone for a while, which Daphne knew was to let her finish working. She appreciated his kind gesture, and the delicious sandwich, and was finally happy with what she'd written. She took great pride in personalising every ceremony she performed so that no two were alike. Of course, most couples these days either wrote their own vows or used ones they'd found – there were so many available online – but it was her part which gave an extra special touch.

When couples booked her services she sent them a comprehensive questionnaire in order to better understand who they were as people and as a couple. Everything from how they met to the proposal and so much more. Using that information and then meeting them, she could craft a meaningful ceremony which included their own special words to each other.

She had Arvin's questionnaire printed out. Belle hadn't completed one which Daphne now knew was thanks to Arvin's secret plan. He'd kept some things to himself in order not to give away Belle's identity but Daphne had made plenty of mental notes since the truth was revealed. Until the happy couple read it all later today, she wouldn't know if she'd nailed it.

I think I have.

Daphne washed her plate then stepped outside to let John know she was done.

But where was he?

His fishing gear was in its usual place. And so was the car.

Closing the door, Daphne picked a direction, guessing he'd be somewhere near the water. It didn't take long to find him but what on earth was he so focused on? He sat on a bench beneath a tree, empty plate to one side, and phone in front of his face.

But then she saw. The man from last night – Warren – was

arguing with Russell's girlfriend in the carpark across the lake and it didn't sound pleasant. Not that she could catch any words, but they were clearly upset with each other. And her husband was making a video of the encounter, which was both amusing and somehow relieved a little of the guilt she was carrying over the photos she'd taken of the scene at the bottom of the hill. She hadn't squared it with her conscience yet to look at them.

Lainie's arms flew into the air then she spun around and got into her car, slamming the door. A moment later she drove out of the carpark at speed.

Daphne had stopped so as not to interrupt John but now she crossed the short distance to join him, just as he lowered the phone. He rolled his eyes in the direction of Warren, who'd lit up a smoke again.

'What was that all about, love?'

'Your guess is as good as mine. They were kissing. Then started arguing. Couldn't hear a word but something isn't right between them. How's the ceremony going?' He stood and collected his plate.

'Hang on... they were kissing? Oh dear, do you think Russell knows?'

'Not sure it's our place to tell him. So, the ceremony?'

'All done, at least until the happy couple see it.'

Arm in arm, they strolled toward Bluebell.

'I don't know what to make of it all,' Daphne said. 'For a police officer to be present at the scene of a death – suspicious or not – yet do nothing about witness statements or more than a cursory examination of the body... it doesn't sit well with me.'

'I agree. All I can imagine is the shock of his friend dying affected his training and knowledge. They'd just been out for dinner and expected to get back in a car together to leave.'

All of Daphne's senses told her something was off. Yet the police were unconcerned and there'd been no mention that the crime scene unit had found anything untoward.

'On a more pleasant subject,' John said. 'What are your

thoughts about having dinner at the winery tonight? It's very kind of Susan to invite us to come back.'

Exactly where was Susan when Godfrey fell?

'I'm happy to go. If you are? Unless there's another place which appeals?'

'Lots, actually. But I'm also keen for us to spend as much time around Belle as possible, now we've found her.'

'Or she found us. Arvin, anyway. I might make a few notes before the lovebirds arrive, if you don't mind?'

'Not at all. I noticed we're a bit low on coffee so will take a walk into town to buy some. We can make a list.' John opened Bluebell's door and ushered Daphne in.

Aren't we the cutest couple? Real grey nomads.

There really was nothing better than the new life they'd made for themselves.

Once John had left, with quite a long list of shopping, Daphne watched the video he'd taken. She liked the function their phones had of dropping photos and files to each other with the press of a button.

Sadly, the distance was a bit too far to even try and lip-read the conversation between Warren and Lainie – not that she was an expert, but she'd picked up a few skills over the years and usually managed to identify a few words here and there. What was obvious was the agitation from Lainie but there was no reason to believe the meeting was concerning Godfrey.

She opened her notebook and scribbled a paragraph or two describing the video, including the time it was made, the date, and location.

Then she turned to her notes from late last night after they'd returned from the winery, glad she'd worked on them while so much was fresh in her mind because after the visit with Belle and Arvin earlier, there was a lot to add.

- Susan at restaurant until two in the morning doing deep clean
- Belle not thrilled that Marsha took over from Tori (who had a motorcycle accident)
- Arvin and Claude Benoit arguing
- Claude telling Belle to ask Russell why he is so upset
- Russell says strange stuff about Belle deserving to be married to the head winemaker and Claude expecting to leave
- Constables Joyce Woodcroft and Perry Freeman say they thought Jeremy had taken care of statements last night
- After Eddie's accident, the bookkeeper embezzled funds which were mostly recovered by Godfrey, acting as the estate's lawyer
- Community rallied to help winery recover
- Letters...

What is the story with these letters?

Heather's interruption had come at the worst time, leaving Daphne without vital information. Because by now, having finished her notes and reread the previous ones, she was convinced there was a dark cloud over the winery. Ever since Eddie's accident there'd been moves to harm the reputation, the finances, and even the grapevines which had made Crystal Springs so successful. What if the accident was actually part of a bigger plan?

But what could Godfrey's death have to do with it, other than his past role as lawyer and marriage to the head chef? Neither of those were current.

And who could possibly benefit from his death, or the fallout from Eddie's accident?

Grabbing her pen, Daphne added a note and underlined it.

Find out who benefits from all of this and you'll find your killer.

She almost ran a line through 'killer'. Jumping the gun wasn't helpful and until there was more information it was also wasting time. Her job here was to perform a beautiful ceremony in two days and ensure that Belle and Arvin began married life in the best way possible. Not solve a crime which wasn't even considered a crime.

Daphne closed the notebook.

THIRTEEN

'Bluebell is beyond adorable,' Belle gushed. She'd worn a huge smile since she and Arvin had parked nearby a few minutes ago.

Seeing her relaxed and happy was a huge relief. There was enough stress on a bride-to-be in the lead-up to a wedding without adding unexplained deaths, ongoing arguments, and changes in the bridal party.

I'll keep her thinking about the big day, not the problems.

Daphne was determined nothing else would mar the wedding. No more snooping or making lists or taking photos.

'There's room for everything.' Belle had peered into the bathroom. 'I've seen much bigger caravans with tiny showers but yours is a nice size. And the kitchen is perfect.'

'Coming from a chef, that's a big compliment,' John said. 'We have a decent barbecue as well which is part of my fish station.'

'And he makes the best fish tacos ever.' Daphne smiled at him. 'Never knew he'd become such a culinary talent on the road.'

'More time to cook now, doll.'

Arvin slid onto the bench on one side of the table and Belle joined him. 'So are you retired?'

John finished making a pot of tea and added it to the cups, milk and sugar Daphne had put out. The two of them sat opposite

Arvin and Belle. It wasn't often they had visitors and it felt so nice... if slightly cramped.

'Not entirely, Arvin. We have a manager running our real estate agency. He intends to buy us out when we're ready but...' He glanced at Daphne. 'But, we have some reservations. There was a complaint about him a while ago and although he was genuinely apologetic and we've had no more worries, our sales are down despite local growth. When we go home this time, I'll do an audit and see where we need to improve.'

It was a worry. They'd owned the premier real estate agency in the region for many years, with lots of return business and an excellent reputation.

'I'd rather not sell until we're back at our best.'

'That's what Mum says about Crystal Springs. Well, it's how she persuaded Dad not to give up,' Arvin said. 'Of everyone, you both would understand how quickly a property can fall in value due to various factors. In our case it was the neglect of the vines... they are the whole reason our vintages are so sought after. We'd lost several staff almost immediately after Dad's accident and it doesn't take long for vines to get hungry or need nurturing. Without Claude working every hour under the sun and the moon I don't think we'd have made it through. He's had several bonuses since we got back on our feet but nothing will really repay his efforts.'

Perhaps he believes he is owed more than just money.

Daphne shoved the thought away. Now was not the time.

'Heather agreed to sell Crystal Springs once it was back to its original value,' Belle said, after a small smile at Arvin. 'But she also said it had to be Eddie's decision because she'd never leave if it was up to her. And last year he finally admitted he wants to keep the property in the family as it has always been.'

'What a relief for everyone.' John finished pouring tea.

'Not everyone.'

All eyes turned to Arvin.

'Only a week after we'd done a press release talking up our

renewed future plans, with me as head winemaker in a few years and announcing the development of the wine lovers' retreat, the first letter arrived.'

Daphne felt her eyes widen.

'Wine lovers' retreat?'

'Didn't I tell you about it, Auntie? It is going to be an incredible place for people who love wine and also want a luxurious, private getaway. They will be able to have personal winemaking sessions, curated gourmet meals, and even play with the horses and donkeys if they want. And the usual massages, beauty therapy, hair, nail and so on. The plan includes a proper spa with a professional masseuse and beauticians and even a dietician who specialises in health.' Belle reached into her handbag and drew out a bundle of envelopes. 'But these letters all warn Eddie and Heather not to pursue it. And now some of the threats are coming true.'

Don't get involved. Do not get excited about this.

Belle took a folded piece of paper from one envelope, opened it, and slid it in front of Daphne and John.

So much for staying out of this. The little skip of her heart reminded Daphne how much she loved putting puzzles together. Well, at least she'd tried to keep her distance.

The letter was typed.

'Looks like this was done on an old typewriter.' John leaned closer to inspect. 'Typeface is a bit uneven as well.'

There were only a few lines but the words sent a chill up Daphne's spine when John read them aloud.

Was almost loosing your life not enough, Ed?

Think your some kinda superstar with your fancy plans.

Gold medals wont save CS.

Time to sell if you know whats good for you.

'Yep, definitely used a typewriter because a computer program would've fixed all the grammar.' Daphne was trying to lighten the mood but the lack of apostrophes and other errors might help narrow down the author. 'Gold medals being for wines?'

Arvin nodded. 'We've been blessed with a number over the years.'

'I thought the local wineries were all supportive of each other?' John asked.

'They are. Dad's certain these aren't from a competitor.'

Belle made a pile of the remaining letters. 'Shall I read?' She picked up the top one.

Nobody likes losers.

You are a loser. Lost walking. No standing. Not a real man.

What will you lose next? Wife? Son? Better think about it.

Time to sell.

'Oh what a dreadful person!' Daphne didn't know whether to cry at the cruelty or scream. Instead, she clenched her hands into fists. 'Poor Eddie.'

There were three more letters, all in the same style. Insulting. Warning. Badly written. The final one was the darkest, with a dire threat that someone would pay the price.

'And there's nothing to identify the sender?' Daphne helped herself to the envelopes, checking the back and front of each. 'A month apart, going by the date stamp. All sent from Benalla.'

'I asked Dad if we could hire a private detective but he brushed it off as being from someone with a grudge.'

'Like the bookkeeper?' John asked.

Arvin shook his head. 'She's serving a prison term. And I think their mail gets checked before posting. There were several staff who left abruptly when they found out it might be months, if at all, before Dad was back. But that was more about their job security fears and each was properly paid out.'

Belle reached her hands across to take Daphne's. 'Please will you help us solve this?'

'I'm not sure I can, dear. Not through lack of wanting but if the police have already said there's nothing to be done…'

'And Daphne and John will be leaving in a few days, babe.'

'I know, Arvin. I just want your beautiful family to get some justice.'

Before Belle could start crying yet again, Daphne squeezed her fingers. 'Tell you what. John and I will have a chat and see if we can come up with any ideas. But in the meantime, we have a wedding ceremony to finalise, so how about we take a look at that?'

Although he understood why Daphne had agreed to look into the letters, John could tell she was uncomfortable with it. Belle was hard to say no to. Always was. He just couldn't see a quick resolution for a long-term problem and Daphne was never half-hearted about anything she did.

He borrowed the letters and took them outside while the other three went through the ceremony.

There, he took a photo of each, returning them to their correct envelope and then photographing those. What good it would do was beyond him but at least they had a copy should they be needed.

It was a pity the police weren't able to do much with them. He'd seen other cases of people writing threatening letters and quite often they became bored or got their anger out of their system, but it was an awful feeling for those on the receiving end. What a pity Jeremy Karlson wasn't more approachable.

John gave his fishing gear a longing look. Sitting on the lake's edge with the water lapping and nothing to worry about other than whether he'd put lettuce or coleslaw in the tacos sounded perfect, yet completely unattainable for the moment.

Bluebell's door opened.

'Have you read the ceremony, Uncle John?' Belle climbed down, eyes bright with tears, but happy ones.

'Not yet. From the look on your face you're happy with it.'

'Ecstatic. Auntie made me cry. Several times. Even Arvin was sniffling away.'

'I was not.' Arvin followed her out.

Belle turned her back to him and mouthed, 'Yes, he was.'

'Don't forget your copies, fresh off our little printer.' Daphne joined everyone and handed Belle and Arvin a folder each. 'There's a copy of the full ceremony as well as your personal vows. The only thing we still need to do is have a walk-through of the wedding. Once we do that, I'll provide a timeline for anyone who needs it. Bridal party. Musicians. Horse handler? Parents. And you both of course.'

'When do you want to do that?' Arvin put an arm around Belle's waist. 'I think we have a bit of time tomorrow morning.'

'Before ten, though. I need to help Susan again and Heather and I are going to collect my dress right after lunch service. There's still so much to do!'

'Can we do anything?' Daphne offered. 'Are your bridesmaids helping?'

Belle made a scoffing sound. 'Sorry. That was rude of me and wasn't directed at Rhianna, who is doing plenty for a woman about to have a baby. Tori was going to collect the gifts we've arranged for each guest but obviously can't, and Marsha is apparently too busy.' She rolled her eyes.

'In that case, leave the gift collecting to us,' John said.

'Oh, are you sure? It's from a shop in Benalla and they'll have them ready early tomorrow morning.'

'We can get those and then meet you at the lake, if that suits?'

Belle threw her arms around John. 'Yes please.'

He patted her back, smiling over her shoulder at Arvin.

'Anything to help.'

After kissing his cheek, Belle stepped back. 'Please come to dinner tonight at the winery? I can do a table for two. Very romantic. And Susan wants to cook you both something special to say thanks.'

Daphne tilted her head. 'Thanking us? Whatever for?'

'For me, actually. Being my parents when I had nobody. Apparently I've barely stopped talking about you since you got here. She knows how hard it was for me at first, living with Dad and having his mother being so negative about my mum. And about you two.' Belle summoned a small smile, but there was pain in her eyes. 'Heather and Susan were much better role models than my grandmother.'

'Of course we'll come for dinner. Please thank Susan for her kindness,' John said.

He felt a bit choked up and had to work hard to keep his voice calm but the minute Arvin and Belle were in their car and driving away, he dropped his guard. And when Daphne burst into tears, he held her against his chest, his own cheeks wet.

FOURTEEN

Daphne insisted John go fishing. They had a few hours until dinner and she wanted to go dress shopping. He'd initially protested as anything he caught couldn't be cooked today, which was his preference, but she turned on the small freezer they had for times such as these and told him to take his time and enjoy the peace and quiet while he could.

They'd both had enough emotion and upset for one day. His reaction to Belle's words was as strong as hers and brought up their old grief at not being able to adopt her.

Hearing that she'd been so unhappy, at least at first, with her father, was doubly distressing and although Daphne wasn't one to wish harm on another person, she was glad Russell's mother wasn't around. Had she been, Daphne would have had some choice words for her. Imagine being so controlling that you'd lie to your own grandchild.

Belle's happy now. Deeply in love, with a strong support system and career.

That was what mattered. And marrying this couple was going to be one of the best days of Daphne's life.

'Do you really think you can pull that one off?'

Her head jerked around at the familiar voice... and mean

words. She was in a fashion boutique on the main street, holding up a light green dress. It wasn't a colour she'd usually wear but the cut was similar to her poor torn blue dress and she had been thinking of trying it on.

Of all the people...

Lainie stood with her hands on her hips on the other side of the counter.

'Oh, hello. I didn't know you worked here.'

It was always better to be pleasant. Particularly to unpleasant people.

'I own the shop. Along with several others. And I'd really not recommend you try to squeeze into such an expensive dress.'

'It is my size, but perhaps you can suggest one more suitable?'

Be nice. She might become Belle's stepmother one day.

'There's a charity shop around the corner.' Lainie stalked over and snatched the dress from Daphne. 'Inexpensive. Suitable for seniors. My clothes are for younger women.'

Right. That was one blow too many, lady.

'Thank you for the recommendation. You must be very busy here.' Daphne pointedly looked around the shop which was filled with stock but had no other customers. 'But if my money isn't as good as all these other people's...' she gestured with a broad smile, 'I shall leave you to look after them all. Have a nice day.'

She let the door close loudly in her wake, heart banging in her chest as she walked briskly away. It wasn't in Daphne's nature to be unkind. Not purposefully. But that woman had gone out of her way to be rude from the beginning and Daphne had had enough of today.

After crossing a couple of streets without paying attention to where she was headed, Daphne finally stopped outside another fashion boutique. She peered through the window to make sure Lainie hadn't run from the other shop to get here first, then slipped inside.

There was soft music playing and a sense of comfort and

welcome. A couple of other people browsed while another chatted cheerily to a young lady behind the counter.

Most of Daphne's attire over the years had either been smart suits for the real estate agency, or comfortable home wear. Since becoming a celebrant she'd gravitated to pants and jackets which were a bit more dressy and a few skirts and dresses for other occasions. Tonight she wanted to look nice for John. He'd seen everything else she owned many times but if they were having a romantic dinner, then she wanted to look the part.

'Special event?' The soft voice beside her was a far cry from Lainie's. It was the young sales assistant who offered a smile. 'You've been looking at this dress for a while and I think it would look lovely on. Would you like to try it?'

A few minutes later, Daphne had paid for not only the dress but a nice scarf, a wide-legged soft pair of dress pants, and a pretty blouse. It was the difference a friendly sales assistant made to a customer and she was excited about dressing up tonight. She decided to let her hair dry naturally after her shower and pin the sides back. And wear her favourite pendant. She ran through her plans as she waited for traffic to pass to cross the road.

It was only as she was crossing that she noticed a business on the other side. A beauty salon which had the words 'For Lease' across the front. On the door was a smaller sign with the name and number of the leasing agent. The door didn't look like it had been opened for a while and there was a pile of mail and newspapers pushed under it.

A single sheet of paper had escaped its envelope.

Something about it drew Daphne's attention but it was too small to read. She got out her phone and zoomed in with the camera, almost dropping it before taking a photo.

'I can't believe it,' she whispered.

Shoulda listened.

You loose.

Your out.

It was typed in exactly the same way as the letters sent to Eddie.

'Another local business being targeted? But it's a beauty salon, not a winery? What on earth is the connection?' John handed Daphne her phone after peering at the screen. 'Any theories?'

I do love a good theory. But where do I even start?

'Not yet, love. But surely the police should be investigating, because it doesn't look like Eddie is specifically the target now. Not unless he ran the beauty salon. Actually, I wonder who did.'

John got to his feet. 'We can discreetly ask around. Do you want to have the first shower?'

She did. Her new dress and all the accessories were laid out on the bed and she was excited about tonight. Their usual routine when going to a new town was to eat out at night and enjoy local cuisine and soak up the atmosphere. So far they'd spent almost as much time at the winery as in Bluebell and very little getting to know Benalla. But even though dinner was back at the same place as last night, this time there was no pressure to meet new people or deal with Russell.

And we might be able to meet Susan and get more intel on last night.

When they drove into the carpark an hour later, it was only half full. Last night the restaurant had been packed until after nine. John opened Daphne's door and offered his hand.

'You look beautiful. I love your hair like that and this dress suits you.'

Even after all these years, his sincere compliment sent a rush of heat into her face. Once out of the car, she did a little twirl, loving the feel of the fabric against her legs.

His smile lit up her heart and she kissed him on the lips, giggling and stepping back as headlights approached.

'I'll stay out of the bushes and trees tonight. This dress isn't going to be ruined like the last one.'

John gave her a comical look of disbelief which made her laugh again, and then arm in arm, they wandered up the steps.

Kenny was at the front desk and didn't look at all happy or welcoming although he was polite. His eyes darted behind them and then around the room, which was sparsely seated.

'There's a table ready for you, if you'd follow me.'

He collected menus and led the way to the table where they'd sat this morning. Now, though, it was set for two, with delicate flowers in a small vase and a warm flickering candle. It was beside the window and furthest from the door, in a corner, with no other diners nearby.

'I understand Susan is coming to speak with you momentarily about her menu so I will let you look at the drinks options and send a server over.'

Kenny scurried back to his desk, eyes still scanning everywhere around him.

'Is it just me, or does he seem jumpy?' Daphne asked.

'Very jumpy. Not surprising after last night.'

Daphne's phoned beeped a message. 'Sorry, I'll quickly see who this is. Oh, Constable Woodcroft. She asks if I can come in to make a statement tomorrow.'

'Oh goodness, it will be tight timewise, doll.'

'Hmm. The morning is pretty much taken up. We could drop into the police station on the way back from doing the walk-through tomorrow. That way we get the rest of the day to ourselves.'

'Good thinking.'

She tapped out a reply, adding that she'd have a better idea of timing in the morning.

The response was fast.

'She says, *yes, please let me know closer to the time to ensure either myself or Constable Freeman is available. There have been some developments regarding Mr Goffin so we are scheduling a number of people to give statements.'* Daphne looked up. 'What developments?'

'I think I can help with that.'

Susan had approached the table unnoticed and offered a tight smile.

'While I wholeheartedly welcome you back, I'm also a tad worried the evening may be cut short. As it is, more than half of tonight's bookings cancelled, presumably because of what happened here.' After sharing a proper introduction, Susan continued. 'Apparently Godfrey's death has been escalated to the coroner and quite honestly, it should have been from the start. He knew the grounds well and wouldn't just fall down a hill, not even if he was drunk, which he wasn't.'

The hairs stood up on Daphne's arms.

The photos I took... I might need to show them to John. Maybe the police.

She'd not looked at them since that night. Not even on the night. Just snapped away until people started arriving. For all she knew there was nothing in those shots other than branches or dried leaves on the ground.

'Do you believe he was pushed?'

'I don't know what to think, Daphne. This all looks dreadful for the restaurant. The winery. And just after he'd posted that revolting review and people saw me have words with him. I might be the main suspect.' Susan's face was unreadable. 'But hopefully, we'll get through service without any arrests. After consultation with Belle I've created a menu for you both which we hope you'll enjoy.'

She spoke to one of the servers on her way to the kitchen.

'Puts a bit of a damper on things.'

'But did *she* do it?' Daphne asked.

'Did Susan murder Godfrey?'

Daphne nodded.

'It seems unlikely. Her concern for the reputation of the business seems genuine to me. Even if she is capable of killing someone, why do it here?'

Susan. Knife.

That's what Godfrey muttered with almost his final breath. And those injuries to the man's neck and head... was there a chance a blade was responsible? And hadn't Susan been doing a deep clean of the kitchen that same night?

'Oh dear. I'm hoping you're right, love. We both know how quickly fingers can point at an innocent person. Susan seems such a nice woman and our Belle completely trusts her. That has to count for something.'

As the server approached, Daphne glanced at her reflection in the window. Was it all still just speculation on the part of the police? Just for once, couldn't there be a wedding without a scandal?

FIFTEEN

Although the three-course meal was delicious, John got the impression Daphne wasn't even tasting the food. The conversation with Susan had got under her skin and while he was worried about what might happen next, something more was bothering his wife. He knew her too well and after dessert, as they waited on coffee, he decided it was time she let him in on her thoughts.

'Two minds are better than one,' he said.

She blinked. 'O-kay.'

'A problem shared is a problem halved.'

The corners of her mouth twitched.

'It takes two to tango.'

Okay, that last one was pushing it.

At least Daphne was smiling.

He reached across the table and took one of her hands. 'What I'm trying to say is I can see you are mulling something over. And you know there is nothing you can't discuss with me.'

'Other than plans for your birthday.'

'A surprise party?'

'Not another word.' She pretended to zip her lips. But then her face fell and her grip on his fingers tightened. 'There is something you don't know. Actually, nobody does. And I'm not very proud of it, but at the time I was overcome with a need to do something. Anything.'

This might be worse than he'd expected but John kept his gaze steady. 'Go on.'

She looked around and then nodded, more to herself than him. 'There's something I need to show you but not in here. On my phone. Back in Bluebell.'

'Sounds a bit cloak-and-dagger.'

'I don't know what I was thinking. I'll probably delete them.'

Photos? Oh... did you take photos when you were with Godfrey?

He was a patient man and would wait until they were home rather than press her now. The coffee arrived, each with a locally made chocolate on the saucer. No wonder the restaurant was – usually – so popular. Every bite of every dish had been perfect.

'Maybe the person writing the letters is winning.' Daphne sighed deeply and released John's hand to stir her coffee. 'Didn't Susan say more than half the bookings for tonight cancelled? The effect of Godfrey passing away must have affected the town in more ways than one. But what if he was simply collateral damage?'

'How so?'

'Maybe he was in the wrong place at the right time for the killer. It might have been any one of us who became the victim. We might have met the person. Sat at the same table. Been served by them.' Daphne's head gestured toward Kenny, who was staring out of the window into the dark.

It was an interesting, if disturbing, suggestion. Someone who had had enough of being ignored by Eddie despite the growing demands in their letters. If it was someone close to the winery then that opened a whole other can of worms.

'We shouldn't get ahead of ourselves. After all, the coroner is the person everyone needs to wait on unless there's other evidence. And the crime scene unit was here for some time so there's a lot to be done. We'll be long gone before much else happens.'

The front door opened and several police walked in, one after another. One of them was Jeremy Karlson and he stared straight at Daphne and John.

'Uh-oh. I think I spoke too soon.'

At first the police officers stood just inside the door as though waiting to be seated. But nobody came to speak to them. Kenny had vanished in the last couple of minutes since Daphne last looked and the other servers were busy with tables.

'Listen up! I want to talk with management. Now.'

Jeremy's voice boomed louder than the background music and chatter and people collectively turned, startled, to look at him. One server hurried in his direction while another almost ran to the kitchen. Somebody turned off the music and a strange hush descended.

Daphne's eyes moved from the police to the kitchen door which was still swinging behind the server. Who was in there other than Susan, Belle and the rest of the kitchen team? Kenny must be. And the server. But why was nobody coming out? Kenny and Susan were the only management here and as the seconds ticked by, their absence became more noticeable. And alarming.

A few people stood, making ready to leave.

'John, get your phone out. Start recording,' Daphne whispered.

He was in a better position to do so discreetly and something told her it mattered to keep a record of what was happening. She moved a bit to shield him from the view of the police.

Jeremy turned his attention to the remaining server, who was hovering around the desk in a bit of a flap. 'Where's Kenny?'

'Bathroom.'

'And Susan?'

'Bathroom.'

'They can't both be at the bathroom at the same time!'

The poor man shrank back.

'Do I have to do everything myself?' Jeremy stalked toward the kitchen and almost reached it when Belle and Susan emerged.

Belle hurried toward John and Daphne but Susan planted herself across the doorway, arms crossed and legs apart.

'Where's Kenny?'

'Bathroom.'

'Let me past.'

'Do you have a warrant?'

Other people had their phones out, some making calls and others taking videos. Even the constables stopped what they were doing to watch the standoff.

'I have cause to look in the kitchen.'

'I seriously doubt that, Jerry.'

'Don't test me, Susan.'

'Love, we need to do something.' Daphne was on her feet.

John's hand snaked out to grab her arm. 'We are.' He was still recording.

She sat again, her toes tapping the floor in a nervous reaction. Belle arrived, squatting at her side.

'He's trying to pin Godfrey's death on Kenny or Susan, or both,' she whispered. 'Poor Kenny is terrified of him.'

Understandable. The police officer used his height advantage to stand over Susan but, unlike Kenny, she wasn't fazed.

'Officer, unless you have a warrant then I am asking you to leave. This is private property and you might recall I was once married to a lawyer. I know our rights.'

'Oh I bet you do. Did you murder your ex-husband? I think you did.'

One of the other guests gasped at those words and for the first time, Jeremy noticed he was being recorded by multiple people. His face darkened further and he lowered his voice so only Susan could hear. She jerked her head back and even across the distance, her face drained of colour. But she didn't relax her stance and Jeremy stormed back to the front desk.

'We're leaving.'

He didn't wait for anyone, flinging the door open and disappearing into the night.

'Sorry, everyone. Thanks for cooperating.' Constable Wood-croft was next out of the door, followed by the other two officers.

Belle immediately ran to the front desk to hug the poor server. People began lining up to leave.

'I've got all the footage.' John slid his phone into a pocket. 'Might be worth sharing it with Eddie and Heather in case they need to speak to a lawyer but I reckon there'll be plenty of video posted on social media tonight.' He grinned. 'People are quick to reach for a phone these days.'

Heather and Eddie arrived, with him heading in the direction of the kitchen. Heather spoke to Belle briefly then made an announcement.

'There's no charge for anyone. We can't possibly ask you to pay after such a disruption.'

To the credit of the guests, only one couple walked out without stopping to pay, the rest refusing to go until they had. It gave Daphne a bit of hope for humanity.

'I'd really like to check that Susan is okay. Do you think we can go into the kitchen?' Daphne hadn't seen Susan go back through the door but she wasn't there when Eddie reached it. What a brave woman she was, standing up to a bully wearing a uniform. 'Maybe we should ask Belle once she's free.'

John offered Daphne his hand and they made their way to the front desk, waiting a bit to one side as the final guests left. Heather went to lock the door but then held it open to let Arvin in. He threw his arms around her and she said something like, 'Ew, you smell bad' and pushed him away. Then he did the same with Belle.

'My babe. My bride. You were almost arrested.'

'Good grief, how drunk are you?' Belle laughed as she extracted herself. 'And nobody was arresting anyone. Go and sit down and I'll find some water.'

'Not drunk, darlin'. Just happy. Gonna be marrying my pretty lady soon.' But Arvin did flop onto a chair with the silliest of grins. He waved to Daphne and John. 'Hello, in-laws.'

A little bubble of joy lifted Daphne's spirits.

'He's been out with his groomsmen,' Heather said. 'How did you get here?'

'My boys. Mates, yeah. Dropped me. But not drinking. Not Owen.'

'But how did you even know? That the police were here?'

He frowned while he thought about it. 'Pub. Someone saw a video. Told Owen. He said we'll get going. Can I have a beer?'

Belle returned with a bottle of water. 'Here you go. A nice cold beer.'

'You are the best. Best bride.'

She rolled her eyes and gestured for Daphne and John to follow her away. 'Would you come and see Susan? She's a bit agitated.'

'Is Arvin okay to leave there?' John asked.

'Heather's going to cash up the register so she'll watch him. Poor love, having to cut his night short. But it might be for the best if he's already wasted.'

As they followed Belle, John looked a little puzzled.

'Drunk, love. Wasted means quite inebriated.'

'I must be getting old.'

The swinging door led to a short hallway. On one side were bathrooms and a staff room and on the right was an 'in' door and an 'out' door to the kitchen. And at the end of the hall was a fire door, which was propped open.

The kitchen was much larger than Daphne had imagined, with lots of stainless steel benches and enough appliances to prepare food for an army. And knives. So many knives, all neatly lined up along a magnetic strip.

Susan sat on a low stool on the servers' side of the pass, head in her hands and shoulders heaving. Eddie was right beside her, awkwardly patting her arm and talking to her.

'None of this is your fault, Suse.'

'It is, though.' A sob. 'It's my fault Godfrey's dead. My doing.'

SIXTEEN

Daphne couldn't believe her ears. Surely she'd misheard? But a quick glance at John's shocked face told her there was nothing wrong with her hearing.

Susan. Knife.

Godfrey's words haunted her.

There was an abundance of knives in here.

It didn't make sense. Daphne was a good judge of character. Excellent, actually. At least most of the time. Her intuition couldn't reconcile this warm and caring woman with being a cold-hearted killer.

Eddie noticed the three of them and his expression was one of pure relief. 'Come on, Suse, we have company.'

She sighed heavily and lifted her head. Her face was streaked with tears which she tried to brush away with her hands. Daphne always had a travel-size packet of tissues in her bag and quickly handed them over.

'Why do you think Godfrey's death is your doing?' Daphne had to ask. She needed to know what was going on in the other woman's mind.

'The knives. It was my idea to put all except my personal ones on the magnetic board and that just means anyone could come in here and take one. We keep the fire door open most of the time so all it would take is someone to pick a moment without one of us in here. I don't really know but Kenny told me when he was doing CPR he got a close look at two injuries and was pretty sure one was a stab wound. I guess it might have been from something else but a knife came to mind.'

'Are any missing?'

'That's the weird thing. None are. I've double-checked the magnetic board.'

Belle had collected more bottled water and shared them around, and then she started dragging stools from the staff room. John went to help and by the time Susan had dried her face, they were all seated in a circle of sorts. Everyone was quiet, waiting for someone to start talking. The silence dragged. Daphne wasn't good with silences.

'I love this kitchen.'

'So do I,' said Belle.

'Best I ever worked in.' Susan gazed around. 'I walk in each day and admire it. Making good food is easy in here.'

'You could make a gourmet meal on a campfire,' Eddie said with a grin. 'Next to Heather, you are the best chef I've ever had the pleasure of knowing. And Belle is right up there as well.'

'Well it certainly helps having the perfect workspace.'

More silence.

Water was drunk.

This really isn't getting us anywhere.

'Why so quiet? Are we praying... whoops, no offence, anyone.' Heather held the door open. 'I'm just going to put this in the safe and really, really could use a glass of wine.'

Then she was gone, the door closing behind her.

'Wine is an excellent idea,' Eddie said. 'Belle, do you mind?'

'I'll help.' John stood. 'Let Heather have this seat and I'll get another on the way back.'

Before silence could reign for the third time, Daphne decided to keep things light. 'Our dinner was wonderful, Susan. I've been experimenting with tart pastry and I think I'm not too bad – according to my generous husband that is – but yours was so light with the sweet ricotta and plum filling. I can't seem to roll mine so thin.'

'I'd suggest you get Belle to show you because those were hers, but with the wedding she might be a bit busy. But there'll be other times, now you've reconnected?'

'Oh, I do hope so. She said to me she still dreams about our little town by the sea.'

'Russell has a lot to answer for.' Eddie's words came out abruptly. 'For a smart businessman he is easily led. His mother was behind him never being part of Belle's life from before she was born and these days he listens to Lainie over everyone else. Recently he keeps saying he wants nothing but the best for his daughter but back then... well, he backed up his mother in the lie about not being allowed to contact you both. It crushed Belle when she found out it wasn't the case but she's one to forgive quickly.'

Daphne gestured as Heather returned. 'There's a seat here. Belle and John are getting wine and an extra stool. May I ask where Arvin is?'

Eddie looked surprised. 'He's at the pub.'

'No, he's on his way to the house, being helped by Owen. Apparently there's a video doing the social media rounds of Jeremy Karlson throwing his weight around here and Arvin insisted on coming to help... even after consuming more than enough beer. Owen dropped him back then decided to check he'd made it up the steps okay,' Heather said.

'He'll have a headache tomorrow,' Eddie chuckled. 'Wine he can drink like the future head winemaker he is, but not beer.'

'Please wake him early though.' Belle was back, carrying a bottle of wine and several glasses. 'We have a full day.'

'Don't worry, honey. I'll pop the washing machine on which is against the wall of his bedroom. And if that doesn't work I'll send the cats in. You know they adore him. Especially around breakfast time. *Wake up, hooman. Wake u-up.*' Heather winked at Belle.

John wheeled in a stool for himself and collected his bottle of water while Belle poured wine for the rest of them.

'Thanks, honey. This will hit the spot.' Heather raised her glass. 'To working out what the heck is going on.'

'And making sure my wedding goes as planned!'

Everyone took a sip, John of his water.

'Have your staff all gone home?' Daphne suddenly realised there was nobody else here.

'There's only some washing up to put through the machine which I'll manage before I leave,' Susan said. 'Kitchen hands went early as did most of the line cooks. Not enough customers tonight to warrant keeping them here.'

'There were two servers before. And Kenny.'

Susan was suddenly interested in her glass of wine, staring into it as though she'd not heard.

Daphne turned her attention to Belle, who did a kind of wriggle in her seat and tried to look away but couldn't. She'd never been able to keep things from Daphne. 'We sent everyone home. Poor Mike was talking about quitting after that horrible Jeremy yelled at him.'

'What? I'll phone him. Actually, I'll message him now, with it being so late, and we can talk tomorrow.' Eddie looked worn as he tapped on his phone.

It wasn't fair. These were good, salt-of-the-earth people who'd worked hard their whole lives and almost lost everything thanks to a tragic accident. Then some cruel person decided to target them while they were still recovering. Who would do such a thing? And just as important... why?

'Where's Kenny though?' Daphne asked quietly. 'John and I observed him during the evening and he seemed jumpy. On edge. We thought it was a result of the tragedy last night but I noticed him looking out of the window just before the police arrived and then he disappeared. Belle, you told me earlier he is terrified of Jeremy.'

She could have sworn Belle mouthed 'sorry' to Susan. Interesting.

'Just between us,' Heather said. 'Kenny was a police officer. A long time ago. We've known him since he was a youngster. He even worked here during school holidays as a teen, as many of the local kids have over the years, making some extra money and helping us with a harvest or some other job. He always wanted to join the police though and went through academy, then was posted at a station up north.'

Eddie put his phone down. 'After about a year, maybe a bit more, he wandered in one day and asked if we had any work going. Said the force wasn't right for him. We were happy to have him. We needed a waiter and over time he grew with the role and became maître d'. He's good at his job and popular with the customers.'

'About five years ago, Jeremy Karlson and his brother Warren came for dinner with Russell and Godfrey. I was still head chef. Kenny came rushing into the kitchen, barely able to get a word out. Turns out Jeremy was his senior officer up north and although he never explained what happened, I guess he was the reason Kenny resigned. I'll never forget how nervous he was about running the restaurant that night.' Heather shook her head.

Susan was back staring at her wine, which she'd barely touched.

You know more than you're saying.

'Did you know Jeremy?' John asked.

'Not until then. He'd just transferred to Benalla but he knew Godfrey and Russell through Warren, who already lived here.'

Susan abruptly got to her feet, her stool almost scooting away before Belle steadied it. 'This kitchen won't clean itself so please excuse me.'

'I'll help.'

'No, you will take a break, young lady. It's bad enough you are doing lunch service the day before your wedding but you don't need to be working late tonight.' Susan came back and kissed

Belle's cheek. 'If it's quiet again tomorrow then the girls and I will manage everything.'

'We should have closed tomorrow,' Heather said.

'I'm only doing lunch and then, you and I are going to collect my wedding dress tomorrow. You know I like to keep busy.'

The love between Heather and Belle, and Susan and Belle, touched Daphne. Having such strong and kind women as role models mattered. Much better than that awful Lainie Newman.

'Can I ask an odd question?'

'Odder than both dinners you've had here?' Eddie's smile was wry.

'I noticed a shop which was closed down in town. A beauty salon. Up for lease.'

'Oh.' Belle's face dropped. 'Tori used to work there.'

'Tori did?'

'She was one of three beauticians including the owner. The day after her accident, her boss closed the shop. No idea why. Tori still doesn't know what happened and is owed a bit of backpay because the owner left town abruptly. So weird because it was a great little place for a facial or whatever. Very popular.'

Too popular? Was it in someone's way? Just like Crystal Springs?

Eddie had an accident. So did Tori.

Threatening letters. Was Godfrey yet another 'accident' or... was it possible that he'd been responsible for what happened to Eddie and to Tori and someone close to them both decided to take matters into their own hands?

Daphne gazed at the people in the kitchen. Susan. Eddie. Belle. Heather. Even Arvin. None of them were killers. Surely not.

SEVENTEEN

John was fast asleep, snoring softly in their bed. Daphne had no hope of slumber, no matter how tired her body felt. She'd tried to settle but an overactive mind forced her to sneak out of bed and close the curtain between the bedroom and living areas, hoping not to disturb him.

Opening her notebook to the last dot points she'd written, she began adding more. While her thoughts were fresh was the best time to record the most recent events and it didn't take long to have a whole new list. Surely somewhere in here were quality clues which would lead to... what?

There had been no formal declaration from the police that they were investigating a murder, apart from Jeremy's accusation that he believed Susan was responsible. Godfrey's body was with the coroner, a process which might take days or weeks to yield an outcome. Any forensic evidence would likely take months. So was there a clear indicator the man had suffered harm from another person?

Maybe I have evidence.

For the first time since taking them, Daphne looked at the photographs.

When the police had considered the death a sad accident

there'd been no reason to show anyone. Not even John, who'd still not seen them thanks to the two of them being exhausted tonight.

There were lots more than she recalled taking.

She put down the phone and got a glass of water, standing at the window while she sipped and tried to settle a sudden rush of panic. Had she made a dreadful mistake? Not just by taking the photos – which on its own was a questionable move – but by then not sharing them with the police as a matter of urgency?

Before she could overthink things, she sat again and started scrolling.

Tears formed in her eyes as she looked at Godfrey's face... there was no life there, no matter how hard poor Kenny tried to revive him.

Pull it together, Daph.

There were indeed plenty of images of bushes and dried leaves and the ground and even one of the sky bordered by tree tops. But she'd managed to capture some close-ups of Godfrey's injuries. Somehow she kept her hands from shaking too much and selected a handful to show John in the morning.

Her memory hadn't failed her. A narrow wound in his neck was likely the source of most of the blood. Daphne was not a doctor. Nor a nurse or paramedic. But she'd done several advanced first-aid courses as well as watched numerous documentaries about true crime. This narrow cut was close to – if not into – the anterior jugular vein. And then there was the second wound, this time to his skull.

She distinctly recalled telling Jeremy there was a cut and he'd said she was imagining things. What else did he say? Something about only seeing a skull injury and that it was probably from a fall. He'd jumped to that conclusion without proper consultation or even a look under decent light. In fact, it was raining at the time so visibility was even more restricted. And he hadn't questioned how that puddle of blood got onto the path.

She'd put his responses from the evening down to shock at the sudden death of his friend, but now she wasn't so sure.

Daphne let herself out of Bluebell, taking her phone and very softly closing the door. Their chairs and outdoor table were set up beneath the extendable annexe awning and she sat down to think.

In a few hours she'd get the chance to make an official statement about the evening Godfrey died. Answer any questions the police had. Show them the photographs. Recount his final words. Except, what if those words led to Susan? Not only had he spoken her name, but he'd said the word 'knife' and surely a cut small and precise enough to open an artery could well be from the blade of a professional chef's knife. Daphne sighed audibly and gazed into the night. They might be miles from any other people, so quiet was the camping site.

The emotional rollercoaster of this week was catching up with her. From missing home to reuniting with Belle, then meeting the many wonderful people in her life, seeing Russell again, Godfrey's death. The excitement of the wedding, and most recently the police in the restaurant and the bizarre accusation by Jeremy... what a turmoil.

'I don't know what to do,' she breathed. 'I can't be dishonest but if I tell the police what I heard, and what I know, will Belle ever forgive me?'

She wrapped her arms around herself and let tears silently fall.

After picking up several cartons which were apparently filled with gifts for the wedding guests, John once again drove through the gates to Crystal Springs. Despite Daphne being bubbly and chatty all morning, he knew something was off. He'd woken at one point to find she wasn't beside him and when he'd gone looking, she was outside. And quietly crying.

Normally he'd go and comfort her. Ask what was wrong. Be there for his wife.

But this time his senses told him to let her be.

He'd climbed back into bed and feigned sleep when she came

in a few minutes later. Her hand had reached for his and he'd held it tightly against his chest until she fell asleep.

Despite her broken night, Daphne had woken first and was showered and dressed when he got up. While he followed suit, she made pancakes and coffee, humming away as if she didn't have a care in the world.

Except your heart hurts and your thoughts are troubled.

He'd forgotten about whatever she'd wanted to show him last night, being exhausted all of a sudden when they arrived home. And this morning she'd been a hive of activity getting ready to go out. If he wasn't wrong, her sadness during the night was tied to her secret.

'Oh, there's Arvin and Belle. And their bridal party! Goodie, we can do a full run-through.'

Daphne pointed toward the lake and John slowly bumped the car over the grass to park beside a few others. A dozen or so seats were laid out to make an aisle from near the boathouse to where a low podium was partly constructed. More seats were folded in a pile and there was much to be done to finish the area.

'It really is beginning to feel like a wedding, love.'

'I'll drop you first and take the cartons to the restaurant.'

'Or we can do that last? I wouldn't mind a quick word with Susan before we go to the police station.'

Ah... you're worrying about what Godfrey said before he died. What a conundrum.

Once out of the car it was clear there were more people here than first thought. Russell, for one, which made sense if he was giving Belle away. And Lainie.

'Bother.' Daphne's voice was too quiet for anyone else to hear but John.

'You're the celebrant. Chin up.'

'Hi Auntie and Uncle!' Belle almost skipped across to them and planted kisses on both their cheeks. While she was so close she whispered, 'No idea why Lainie is here but try to ignore her.

Apparently she couldn't sleep or something and is in a real mood today.'

'We'll be fine, dear. This morning is all about you and Arvin. Now, what if I have a word with the two of you first, just to confirm a couple of points?'

Belle and Daphne headed in the direction of Arvin, who was wearing dark sunglasses and had a bit of a seedy look. John wasn't sure where to go. He wasn't part of the ceremony, although had life worked out differently it would have been him walking Belle down the aisle. A dart of regret made him change direction. A walk around the lake was in order.

It wasn't huge, covering an acre or two, but was a pretty and restful area. There were reeds in a couple of spots to give waterbirds hiding places and large lily pads with the last of the summer flowers enjoying a final bloom. Two old willows gracefully drifted their branches into the water and the occasional splosh at the surface confirmed his guess that there were fish. How pleasant to take a rowboat out to the middle and have a floating picnic. Or even a nap. He yawned.

There was a bench beneath one of the willows and from there John could see Daphne and the others. It seemed like a good place to stop a while and watch his wife do her job.

'Let's go through it again and this time I'll stand near the podium and let everyone do their thing.'

This was their third run-through and Daphne was confident it was the last. Belle was on top of things and Arvin – as hungover as he was – had already picked it all up. He stood near her now, still wearing the sunglasses. He'd been chugging water from a huge container between practices.

People moved back into position. They could only estimate where Belle would dismount so Russell picked a spot and waited. Someone turned on the music, a beautiful song of love with a nice tempo, that signalled Owen to offer Rhianna his arm and they made their way along the aisle. Brent and Marsha did the same and once all were near the podium, the men stood with Arvin while the ladies took their places on the other side. Rhianna then moved to a seat because Belle insisted she stay off her feet as much as possible.

'Enter the bride,' Daphne called.

Belle pretended to canter to her father, which made everyone laugh. Everyone except Lainie. She stood near the boathouse with her arms crossed, glaring at Russell. He however was enjoying himself and graciously bowed to Belle and held his arm out for her hand. They walked up the aisle and then Russell left Belle opposite Arvin.

'Very good. I did just think though that your dress will need a little fix-up once you're on the ground and someone to give you your bouquet.' Daphne glanced at Rhianna and discarded the idea of the almost full-term matron of honour being given extra duties. And Marsha was more interested in her mobile phone than the proceedings.

'Marsha will do it,' Lainie called. 'She really should be matron of honour anyway, seeing she's fitter.'

'Hey, I'm pregnant. Not incapacitated, thanks.' Rhianna levelled a long look at Lainie. 'And Marsha isn't married so can't be matron of honour.'

Lainie wound through the flower pots to come closer.

'Chief bridesmaid then.'

'You can't have a matron of honour and a chief bridesmaid. There's only the two of us!'

'Listen, Rhianna, it isn't Marsha's fault Belle doesn't have more friends.'

Arvin removed his sunglasses. 'Would everyone stop yelling, please? And I won't have you talk about my bride that way.'

Belle raised herself on her toes and kissed his lips with a quiet, 'Thanks, babe', then smiled at Daphne. 'Susan will do the dress and the bouquet. And Heather. They're going to fuss over me and hand Tilly to one of the staff. Sorry, should have let you know. So

I'll need maybe thirty seconds or a minute extra before starting the walk.'

Lainie abruptly stopped with a comical look of horror. '*Susan?* Why would you have a cook look after such an important part of the day? Of any part of a wedding? And particularly *her?*'

There was a shocked silence. Belle paled. Arvin took her hand. Even Marsha looked up from her phone.

'Because I love her, Lainie,' Belle managed. 'She's my mentor and almost as much a mother as I feel Heather is. Almost as much as Daphne is.'

Tears threatened to appear from nowhere and Daphne quickly dug up her sunglasses and switched them for her normal glasses. Goodness, this was turning into a mess instead of being a simple walk-through. Time to get it back on track.

'How about we finish up now? I think everyone knows their part. And most importantly, that we're all here for Arvin and Belle. All of us.' Wishing she'd left her glasses on so Lainie would get the message with a stern stare, Daphne was ready to defend the couple any way she had to.

Be mean to me as much as you want but don't you dare upset my girl.

'Say something, Russell. Don't let these people gang up on me.' Lainie's voice was whiny.

The way Russell squirmed, he probably wanted the ground to swallow him. His face was red and he didn't look at anyone. 'I've got a meeting in half an hour. Might head off. Coming, Lainie? Marsha?' He briefly lifted his eyes to meet Belle's. 'Sorry, kid.' Then he was off, striding across the grass without a backward look.

Lainie tore after him, catching him halfway to the car and clearly giving him an earful of her grievances.

Marsha rolled her eyes. 'She never stops. See you in the morning for hair and makeup?' This was directed at Belle, who kind of waved and nodded. 'Bye, then.' She took her time catching up and the second she was in the car, it started and drove away.

Belle flopped onto a seat near Rhianna. 'I don't want her here tomorrow. Lainie, that is. Please tell me there's a way to uninvite her?'

EIGHTEEN

Once John parked in the carpark the groomsmen descended to help carry the cartons up the stairs. Everything was being stored in the staff room and once the restaurant closed after dinner tonight, work would begin to transform the space into a reception room. Daphne had been updating him on Lainie's strange behaviour.

'She really said that?'

'She really did, love. And I didn't mention it but when I went dress shopping yesterday, I ended up in a boutique which she owns. And she was quite unpleasant.'

'You didn't buy that lovely dress from her?'

'Not a chance.'

'I wonder what her issue is?'

I've been wondering that since we first met.

They were back at the car. The groomsmen had driven off. Nobody else was around. Susan wasn't in the kitchen when they'd gone to find her.

'John.'

He gave her a look of mild panic. 'What illegal or immoral thing are we about to do, doll?' His sigh was dramatic, which almost sent her into a fit of giggles.

'Never immoral. Maybe illegal, but I did notice that some of the police tape has broken so I can't see a reason to stop us having a pleasant stroll along the path.'

'I don't think that's a good idea, Daph.'

She hadn't expected him to agree, so had prepared a case to present.

'That nonsense last night with Jeremy throwing around his weight and accusing Susan to her face? Not normal law enforcement behaviour, wouldn't you agree? And it made me ponder why. Why would a senior constable come and harass people with no evidence that anyone there last night had anything to do with Godfrey Goffin's unfortunate demise?'

John watched her intently, which encouraged Daphne to continue.

'If there was evidence that Susan was involved in the murder, then she'd be taken in for questioning, at the very least. But to my knowledge there's been no detectives on the scene, which seems a little strange. Godfrey's body wasn't immediately transferred to the coroner's office and on the night, Jeremy declared it was an accident. Why was he so certain?'

'Just to make sure I understand... you believe Jeremy either had something to do with the death or is covering for someone who did.'

Actually, I hadn't considered he was covering for someone. Good work, John!

'You'll make a celebrant's-spouse-sleuth yet, love. All I know is there's something fishy going on, and I'd just like a quick look in daylight to see if my memory serves me properly.'

'Quick look only. Five minutes tops.'

'Perfect.'

Not willing to risk him changing his mind, she grabbed his hand and tugged until he came with her. Despite his caution, John was grinning. This was better than her 'plan B' if he'd refused. She'd have had to distract him and go on her own and that really wasn't her preference. His opinion mattered.

Both their moods sobered as they stepped onto the narrow

track. Police tape fluttered in the breeze, ending in an abrupt and clean cut.

'This was where I heard him again, love.' Daphne paused, gazing around. 'It was so dark other than the flashlight on my phone. Even in daylight it is spooky.'

'What did you see next?'

'The blood. Well, I knew it was something pooling but until I was almost upon it, blood wasn't what I expected. I have to imagine this is the spot he was stabbed, just from the volume of blood.' She walked to where the blood had been. Now it was nothing more than discoloured, dry dirt. There was a police marker near it: '1'. 'Then I saw his shoe. I stayed on this side to avoid contaminating things.'

Beside a prickly bush was another marker: '2'. 'Is that where you caught your skirt?'

'Look at all the threads. And the police must consider it evidence.' Her chest tightened. What if they thought *she'd* had something to do with the poor man's passing?

Between the pool on the track and where Godfrey had lain were several more markers. Perhaps the crime-scene officers had found more blood or other evidence. There was another area of discoloured dirt and some flattened undergrowth and Daphne stepped away to find a tree trunk to lean against.

'Are you alright?'

'Just a bit upset. It all happened so fast the other night, but now in daylight it feels every bit as real. More so.'

From here Daphne had a different view of where Godfrey had been.

'There's no rocks at all. Just flat ground, apart from the little shrubs he fell onto and those wouldn't have caused the head wound. So where did he get it? Was he hit on the path and staggered here? Or stabbed first?'

'I think we should leave this to the police.'

'You're right, of course. Do you think it's possible for someone to climb down that steep slope from the top grassy area?' She gazed up in the general direction. 'I can see the top. Whatever struck his head might be up there somewhere.'

'Well, speaking for myself, I have no chance of climbing up. What if we take the steps and see if Susan is back?'

'And we can take a quick look on the way. Clever thinking, love.'

'I really wasn't thinking that.'

Daphne was on the move again, this time back the way they'd come. She was sure John muttered something about sleuthing and figured he must be finally accepting his role as her assistant when it came to crime-solving.

The grassy area didn't yield any new information. Under the cover of darkness the other night, Daphne hadn't noticed there was a discreet wire fence to prevent people from accessing the steep descent. The best she could do was peer over the fence in the general direction of where she'd found Godfrey, through trees and past bushes.

'Nothing looks out of place. No broken branches or the like.'

'He'd have had to climb through here first which would tell him it was a bad idea. It seems more likely he went down the stairs and then along the track,' John said.

Turning her back on the view, Daphne nodded. 'My thinking as well. But doesn't that raise other questions? Such as why nobody else saw him out here. And why was he on that path?'

This was one of the biggest parts of the puzzle for her. Several people were outside the building around the time he'd left yet she and John appeared to be the only people who'd heard his moans and that was a while later.

'Be careful there.' Eddie was at the end of the footpath.

'We are.'

They went to join him.

'Arvin tells me Lainie Newman was stirring things up at the practice ceremony.'

'She got a little bit upset,' Daphne said. Better to keep things nice.

With a laugh, Eddie turned his wheelchair. 'Very diplomatic. Are you coming for coffee?'

'I have to go and give a police statement shortly so not right now, but thanks for the offer.' Daphne and John walked either side of Eddie. 'I'd hoped to have a quick chat with Susan first.'

'Let's go and find her. Heather's gone down to give Tilly a bath before tomorrow,' he chuckled. 'I think the poor creature is going to end up with ribbons plaited through her mane. But now I have to come up with a way of suggesting to Lainie she not be here tomorrow or else convince Belle to ignore her. Any suggestions?'

Oh, yes, I have a few. Possibly not the kind you want though.

'Who is close to Lainie and might have a quiet word?' Daphne asked. 'With her daughter in the bridal party and her declaration of expecting to marry Russell, excluding her is problematic. Maybe she could apologise to Belle.'

'She's not the apologising kind. And I don't for a minute believe they'll ever marry. Russell has taken too long to propose and despite his business success he isn't as ambitious as she is or wants him to be. Rumour has it Lainie has her eye on someone else. An old flame, if the gossip is true.'

An old flame she meets near the library?

'Who's that?'

They'd reached the door to the restaurant and John opened it to let the others in.

'No idea. Well, I have my thoughts but will never speak of them. Feel free to go to the kitchen. I need to talk to Kenny about dinner so will leave you to it.'

Kenny was the only staff member in the empty restaurant and he immediately headed over to Eddie.

At the door, Daphne hesitated. 'Feels a bit rude just barging in.'

'Would you prefer we wait until Belle or someone is around?'

'Maybe we should just head to the police—'

'*Nooooo!*' A loud female scream echoed from the kitchen.

John was only a second ahead of Daphne going through first the main door, and then the 'in' door to the kitchen.

Only Susan was in there and she was facing away, angrily folding a long pouch of some kind. There was a glint and Daphne realised they were knives. It reminded her of some cooking shows with professional chefs who brought their own sets with them.

'Are you hurt?' John hurried to Susan's side.

She jumped and snatched up the knife roll, defensively holding it against herself.

'Sorry to startle you. We heard a scream.'

Susan blinked a few times and nodded. 'Goodness. John and Daphne. And how silly of me to overreact, but I just noticed something missing. Something which means a lot to me.'

'One of your knives?' Daphne asked.

'Um... I can't discuss it. A personal matter. Were you looking for me for something? The staff will be here any moment to start lunch service.'

Now what do I say? Your ex wanted me to tell you something? About a knife?

Well of course that's what she needed to do. For some reason, her brain had focused on the words *Susan* and *knife*. But he'd said more.

'I have to make a police statement. We're going there now.'

'You haven't given one?'

'Not yet. And I have to be honest with them about Godfrey's last words, but I believe you need to know what they were as well.'

A flush of colour rose from Susan's neck to the top of her head and she stiffened.

'He said—'

'Morning!'

The door swung open and a parade of staff came in, the last couple laughing about something.

Daphne turned away for a moment as they came in which was

enough for Susan to hurry around the workstation and exit the kitchen.

'Oh goodness...'

She and John followed, finding Susan in the staff room, which was cluttered with the cartons they'd brought as well as heaps of decorations. Susan was twirling the padlock on a locker and gave them a cursory glance.

'Tell the police what you know, Daphne. From everything I know about you, honesty is important, so please don't hold back. Nobody will believe me, anyway.'

'But—'

'I need to start service.'

With that, Susan brushed past.

NINETEEN

'She was struggling to hold back tears and put on a brave face for her team. If only we'd had a few more seconds in the kitchen.'

'I know, doll. But it was like she expected bad news. That Godfrey's last words were somehow going to be an indictment. I wonder if it's because of her conversation with him in the restaurant? It was obvious how angry she was.'

'Mrs Jones?'

Constable Woodcroft appeared in the hallway where John and Daphne sat waiting.

'Please call me Daphne.'

'Would you mind following me?'

'Do you want me to come?' John half-rose.

Daphne looked like she was about to say yes but the constable shook her head. 'Would you mind waiting here? Someone will be along shortly for your statement.'

My statement? First I've heard about that.

He winked at Daphne as she left. She was nervous and still mulling over what information she had to share but knowing his wife, she'd keep to the truth as she understood it.

Heavy footsteps approached. Jeremy Karlson was going somewhere fast. John looked away, hoping to not be noticed. The footsteps stopped.

'Mr Jones, I've made time for your statement.'

Trying not to look as surprised as he felt, John stood and extended his hand to shake. 'Senior Constable Karlson.'

'Actually, it's about to be Detective Senior Constable Karlson. Not official and not widely known so please keep it under your hat. This way, please.'

'Congratulations.'

Jeremy closed the door once John entered the small room. No windows. A wooden table. Two chairs. A lightbulb overhead. He imagined this as an interrogation room with a good-cop, bad-cop scenario going on.

'Please sit. I just want to ask you a few questions and don't have a spare computer to use to type your report as we go. Do you mind a recording instead?' Jeremy placed a tiny device on the table between them. 'One of the juniors will type it up and we'll get you back to sign it.'

'Not an issue, but Daphne and I aren't staying much longer than the weekend.'

This wasn't the original plan but John wasn't comfortable with the events of the past few days and felt a need to get Daphne home to Rivers End ahead of time.

'We'll have it ready before you leave town.' He turned the device on and said his name and John's, the date and time. 'You were present at Pinnacle on Wednesday evening, correct?'

'Correct.'

'What was the reason for your presence and with whom were you attending?'

'My wife Daphne is officiating the wedding of Belle Boyd and Arvin Kingsley tomorrow afternoon. We were invited to have dinner with members of the bridal party and some family members.'

Jeremy crossed his arms and leaned back in his chair while John named each person and their position at the table.

'And how many of these people had you previously met?'

'Arvin, earlier that day. Russell. And Belle, of course.'

'Because you and Mrs Jones were her foster parents in the past?'

'Correct.'

'What is your relationship like with Russell?'

'We barely know him. Until Wednesday evening we'd only met him once, around a decade ago. So there's no relationship as such.'

'You'd have been pretty upset he took Belle from you?'

Where on earth is this going?

'Russell is Belle's dad. It's clear she adores him and that's enough for me.'

Narrowing his eyes, Jeremy leaned forward, placing his arms on the table. 'Do you know that Russell was unaware you were both coming here until just before the dinner?'

'I am.'

'Do you agree that the deception used by Arvin Kingsley was distressing to Russell Boyd and others?'

'Deception?'

'I took a statement from him earlier and he was impressed with how he hired Mrs Jones without the two of you or anyone else knowing he was the fiancé of your former foster child. And people who use deception and lies for their own ends are hardly to be trusted. Yet Mrs Jones is still officiating the wedding.'

Whatever game the man was playing wasn't going to work on John. Over a career in real estate he'd come across all manner of people, both good and bad.

'How is this relevant to Mr Goffin's death?'

'I'll decide what's relevant. But why don't you tell me what you observed on Wednesday, starting with the encounter between Godfrey and Susan?'

This was the strangest conversation John had ever had with a police officer. His eyes flicked to the device on the table. At least anything he said was being recorded and couldn't be twisted.

. . .

Constable Woodcroft tapped away on her keyboard, nodding every so often to let Daphne know she was listening. She was a pleasant young woman, specific with her questions, and patient when Daphne wanted a moment to think.

'Not much more to cover, Daphne. But it is a hard part, I'm sorry. Are you okay to keep going and talk about you finding Mr Goffin?'

'Yes, I'd rather keep going.'

'Good stuff. Let me just see where we're at... Mr Jones had returned to the restaurant to get assistance and you descended the stairs and followed the track. Did you have a torch?'

'Just the flashlight on my phone.'

'And what happened next?'

'I heard a moan and called to him, with no response. As I walked, I came across what looked like blood on the ground.'

'Do you have any medical training? Any qualification in forensics? For the record.'

'I've completed an advanced first aid course. But no.'

The constable added the information.

'Go on.'

'I noticed a shoe and as I got closer, saw Mr Goffin. At that point my skirt snagged on a bush and it took a bit of tugging to free myself. I'm sure I left half the skirt behind.'

I'm not about to admit I was just back at the scene and know your police markers are everywhere.

'Do you still have the skirt? If so, we can get a sample in order to compare to what we found.'

'Of course. I'll pop back with it later.'

'On finding Mr Goffin, what did you do?'

'Actually, before my dress caught, I'd phoned John and told him where I was, that Mr Goffin was injured, and to call an ambulance. Then I approached Mr Goffin and spoke to him.'

Constable Woodcroft's eyes shot to Daphne's.

'You *spoke* to him?'

'I told Jeremy this. Senior Constable Karlson. When he arrived a few minutes later.'

The officer looked genuinely puzzled. Just what had Jeremy kept to himself?

'He actually grabbed my hand. Poor man.'

'And do you recall what you said to him?'

'Yes. It's all very clear in my mind. I told him my name and that an ambulance was coming.'

'I don't suppose... did he respond in any way?' The constable's hands were off the keyboard, her gaze steady.

'He did. I asked where he was injured. I hadn't seen the wounds at that point although there was blood everywhere. That's when he pulled me closer to his face.'

'Did he get any words out?'

If I lie to the police I'm no better than whoever killed him. I promised him I'd find that person but please, please don't let it be anyone Belle loves.

'He asked me to tell Susan something.'

'Wait... Susan Goffin?'

Daphne nodded.

'Tell her what?'

'I'm not certain I heard him correctly.'

'Mrs Jones?'

'He said "knife". His exact words were, "Tell Susan... knife".'

After staring at Daphne for what seemed like minutes, Constable Woodcroft typed rapidly, muttering something under her breath. Then she dropped her hands.

'Did you hear the argument between Godfrey and Susan in the restaurant? After he'd posted the fake review?'

Oh dear.

'We weren't really close enough to hear everything.'

'I've taken quite a few statements today already and two of them mentioned Godfrey asking Susan if she was going to throw a knife at him. She said something about him not tempting her and his reply was that it wouldn't be the first time. Do you recall that conversation?'

Daphne licked dry lips. 'I did hear a comment about her throwing a tea towel at him. He seemed amused. Like it was an old inside joke. They were married, you know.'

'Yes, I know. Did Godfrey say anything else to you?'

'No. He passed away immediately. And I know Kenny did CPR for ages but the man was already deceased. I imagine blood loss had something to do with it. The cut on his neck and wound on his skull. I did tell Jeremy Karlson about those but he looked and said there was only the head wound.'

'You are certain you saw a cut in his neck?'

Wondering if this was her biggest mistake yet, Daphne took her phone out and located the photos she'd taken.

'You might find these useful.'

'I'm sure I've made things difficult for Susan.' Daphne stirred her tea vigorously, sploshing a little onto the saucer. 'Bother. Would you pass me a piece of paper towel, love?'

John did so and joined her at the table as she mopped up the spill.

'I feel the same about my statement. And then there were all those odd questions about the family. First casting aspersions on the motives and honesty of young Arvin, then trying to find out what I know about Eddie and Heather going ahead with the wine retreat.'

'But why ask you?'

'Not that I gave him an answer, but I wanted to ask *him* why.'

Unless he had a stake in it. Or...

'What if he's behind the accidents?'

John almost spat out the mouthful of tea he'd taken. Daphne passed him the paper towel and continued.

'Or the letters. Do you remember one time we were at the police station in Rivers End? It was when Trev Sibbrett was the senior constable there and he had some horrible old typewriter on his desk? There'd just been a power blackout and he found it stored in a cupboard. If one police station has one, surely others might.'

'For what purpose though? What possible interest would Jeremy have in stopping a local business developing new attractions for the town?'

Daphne finally enjoyed her tea while she gave John's questions some thought. Being back in Bluebell was the same as stepping into their house in Rivers End. Comforting. Safe. A haven. Crystal Springs must feel the same to the family who'd lived there for generations. How dreadful to have come so close to losing not only their livelihood, but their home, and all because of a dreadful accident.

'What if the accidents were on purpose?' Daphne reached for the notebook she was using to record her thoughts. 'I made some notes the other night. But at that point we'd been told the death wasn't suspicious. And we didn't know about Eddie's accident, let alone Tori's. I'd love to try and connect some dots.'

Her feelings of letting down Susan, and more importantly Belle, began to subside. Action always helped. But, rather than write, she put down her pen.

'Daph?'

'Belle and Heather are going to collect the wedding dress shortly. Service should be almost over... which reminds me that we haven't had lunch. I'm wondering if we might have a little chat to Arvin. See if we can find out a bit more about this wine retreat and also the two accidents.'

John gave her one of those looks. The kind when he knew she was in full sleuth mode and wasn't sure if he liked it or not.

She smiled as sweetly as she could. 'You know you want to.'

He groaned.

TWENTY

It was almost mid-afternoon by the time they'd had lunch and driven to Crystal Springs. The area around the lake was a hive of activity, with the marquee being erected and the podium and surrounds completed.

'Isn't it lovely that they've set up a marquee for pre-ceremony mingling and drinks?' Daphne said. 'And if that rain returns, at least they can move the ceremony under cover. The boathouse isn't quite large enough.'

'I hope it doesn't rain. Arvin told me he really wants to get some photos of him and Belle in one of the rowboats.'

'Aw, that sounds wonderful! They've really created a beautiful wedding and I'm so excited to officiate it. I can't really believe this is happening, love.' Despite all the negative things taking place, the joy of the next day filled Daphne's heart.

The carpark had only a couple of cars but also a minibus with the words 'Warren's Winery Tours' on its side.

Not Warren from the other night?

They took the stairs and headed for the restaurant. The doors were locked, which wasn't surprising considering it was closed. Daphne peered through the window but couldn't see a soul. 'Where do you think we'll find Arvin?'

'Maybe the barrel room? But for all we know he might be sleeping off the effects from last night, or picking up his suit. Shall I send him a message?' John took out his phone.

'Good thinking.'

While John did that, Daphne wandered along the front of the building in the direction Belle had taken them yesterday. There was a cobbled stone path leading around the outside so instead of going to the stairs, she turned the corner. This side of the building had no windows, but she knew that already from being inside the restaurant. From here it was easy to see through the handful of trees to the cellar door and beyond that, the barrel hall.

'There you are. He says to come down to the cellar door. Where were you off to, doll?'

John took her hand and they turned back toward the steps.

'Just wandering. This is such a lovely property. Do you think whoever sent those nasty letters was hoping Eddie and Heather might put it on the market cheaply, given everything which had happened? Is that a motive?'

'Anything is possible. I have wondered if any of the owners whose properties border this one might be responsible. Horrible thought, but greed sometimes does strange things to people.'

'Another thing to ask Arvin.'

The cellar door was busy, with a dozen or so people at the counter tasting wines. Off to one side, tapping on a phone, Warren Karlson was wearing a top with the name tag of 'Warren' and the same wording as the minibus.

'That's Jeremy's brother from the other night,' Daphne whispered.

John glanced across and the man noticed and waved.

How interesting. So he's in the wine industry too.

Arvin was taking care of a couple, ringing up a sale of a dozen mixed reds and chatting about the weather. He looked completely at ease as he laughed at a comment. His colour was better than earlier in the day, so all that water must have helped. What a dashing groom he was going to be with that ready smile and hand-some face.

A message arrived on Daphne's phone and she almost squealed at the image, quickly showing it to John. It was from Belle, with a photograph of her holding a full-length dress bag against herself.

> I can't wait for you to see this tomorrow! Wish you were here right now. xx.

John grinned and Daphne tapped a reply.

> Cannot wait either, darling girl!

'How wonderful she thought to share with us,' Daphne said. 'I know we will always keep in close touch now we've found her again. And the whole family. Well, Arvin's side at least.'

'I knew you meant that. Russell doesn't seem keen on bridging the gap at all.'

Arvin had noticed them and after a quick word with the other person behind the counter, came around to join them.

'Sorry to make you wait.'

'Nice and busy though.' Daphne smiled. 'If you have customers, we don't mind having a look around while you tend to them.'

'All under control. Everyone is with the tour, so we're just arranging a trolley so that Warren can take all the purchases to the minibus, and my colleague can manage. Why don't we sit under one of the trees nearby? Would you like some water, or a soft drink?'

Bottles of water collected, Arvin led the way to a lovely old Moreton Bay fig tree, its heavy branches reaching wide to offer welcome shade. Beneath was a curved bench where they sat. The grass was lush and birdsong filled the air. From here the cellar door was only fifty or so metres away and soon a procession of people wandered out. Warren followed, pushing a flat trolley packed with wine cartons.

'We hadn't realised Warren was a tour operator,' Daphne said.

'Oh yes, he started off working for Russell, actually. Ran the bar at his pub for a while but he preferred being out and about, so he created his tour business. He's a friendly sort, likes chatting to his clients and knows everyone in the industry.'

'And Godfrey Goffin? I heard he and Jeremy were good friends.'

Arvin nodded. 'Them and Russell. I think Godfrey was Russell's lawyer. Susan would know for sure.'

Except Susan is tight-lipped about a lot.

'The new wine lovers' retreat must be a big job.' John opened his bottle and took a long drink.

'One headache after another, according to Dad.' Arvin laughed shortly. 'We only have a few months to begin construction of the buildings, according to the terms of the council approval. In fact there's quite a few terms we have to abide by, such as the environmental impact and so on, but those were addressed by our builders before Dad's accident. It wasn't easy getting it through the council but Godfrey helped, oddly enough.'

'As your lawyer?'

'Actually, not in a legal capacity. But he was a member of the council and really supportive of the concept. For his faults, the man could see the benefit to the whole town and tipped the scales in our favour, despite some objections.'

That caught Daphne's attention. And John's.

'Our own little town is going through a lot of changes and new developments are sometimes difficult for neighbours. Was that the issue?' His question, phrased from experience, was cleverly worded in Daphne's opinion.

'Not at all. Our neighbours are behind us. We have three and they all wrote letters of support to the council. I don't know who objected, although I'm sure Mum once said Godfrey told Susan while they were still married. Might be worth asking her, if it's of interest?' His eyes narrowed. 'Wait, is this part of your investigation into the letters?'

'We're really not investigators,' Daphne said. 'But whoever sent those letters had a motive, and we wondered if it was to try to push your parents into selling Crystal Springs.'

Arvin leaned back in his seat and gazed upward. 'I love this tree. It was planted by my great-grandmother when the vineyard was being established.' He straightened, his eyes serious. 'This is home to my family and one day I want Belle and I to raise our children here. So does she. Dad's accident and the fallout almost lost us everything and I'm not going to lie: I've wondered if the person who forced Dad's car into a ditch did so on purpose.'

'But why would someone do that?' John asked.

'I don't have a copy because Mum threw it away thinking it was nonsense, but they'd received a letter a few days earlier. It wasn't exactly like the others... not a threat, and rambled on about how Crystal Springs shouldn't diversify with the wine lovers' retreat but focus on making wine. It was just odd getting that then Dad's accident happening. But logically, it was just a terrible incident.'

'The other driver didn't stop?'

'No, and unfortunately our car didn't have cameras installed and there were no witnesses. He barely recalls any of it.'

'I'm so sorry this happened to your family.' John reached over and patted Arvin's shoulder. 'And happy that things turned around eventually.'

Warren wheeled the now-empty trolley back inside the cellar door. On his way out a moment later, he again waved and Daphne waved back. He seemed the opposite of his brother, Jeremy, in nature.

Daphne was itching to ask more questions but Arvin had glanced at his watch a couple of times, so she might need to hurry up.

'It must have been a shock when Tori had her accident. Is she out of hospital?'

'Only just in the last couple of days and she won't be up to attending the wedding, which is a pity.' He suddenly grinned.

'Those three are incorrigible together. Belle, Rihanna, Tori. Really different ladies but they became friends over their love of horses and would do anything for each other.' Arvin stood. 'Sorry, I'll have to run, I still have a lot to do this afternoon.'

'Just before you go... Tori's accident. Belle said her motorcycle was hit by a car?'

'Yeah, a hit and run. They've not caught the driver. Oh. You don't think it was the same person? There's three years' difference, give or take, between the crashes.'

'Just speculating, dear. Now you hurry off and I will see you tomorrow.' Daphne got to her feet and opened her arms to give the young man a hug.

Once he was back inside, she and John cut through the trees to the carpark.

'We have a bit to consider, love. Why don't you do some fishing and I'll make some notes once we're back at Bluebell?'

'Now that sounds like a nice way to spend the rest of the day.'

They were almost back at the car when Daphne's phone rang. 'I don't know this number. Probably one of those spam calls.'

'Might as well answer.'

She did, with a bright, 'Daphne Jones speaking.'

'It's Susan. I need your help, and fast.'

TWENTY-ONE

As soon as Daphne answered her phone, all the colour drained from her face and John took her arm, whispering, 'What's wrong?'

She put the call onto speaker. 'Susan, John's listening as well.'

Susan? He didn't know she even had Daphne's number.

'I'm trying to be calm but a friend who works at the police station told me I'm about to be arrested.' Susan's voice didn't sound calm.

'Arrested!'

'They think I killed Godfrey. I can hear a siren. How ridiculous.'

'Susan, where are you?' John leaned closer. 'Do you want us to come?'

'At home and no. No, what I need is for you to go to my locker at the restaurant. The fire door is always unlocked and my padlock opens with the code seven-three-one. Can you remember that?'

'Seven-three-one, dear. But, whatever for?'

The wail of a siren grew louder through the phone.

'They just pulled up. Please listen. Take everything out of there before the police do. There's an empty crate in the very back of the walk-in freezer which everything should fit into. Just until I can sort this out.'

About to say they couldn't possibly remove evidence, John realised how accusatory it would sound. Nobody believed Susan had killed anyone. Apart from the police.

'Belle said you help people, and I really need help. I didn't kill him. I swear I didn't but somebody wants it to look that way. Seven-three-one. Please.'

The phone call ended and Daphne stared at the phone in disbelief.

'Good grief. What a shock for Susan.' John couldn't imagine how scary police pounding on your door would be.

'Seven-three-one,' Daphne said. She shoved her phone into her handbag and hurried to the steps.

'Hang on. Daph, what are you doing?'

'What Susan asked us to do. Stay with the car, love. I won't be long,' Daphne called over her shoulder. 'Warn me if anyone comes.'

Torn between a lifetime of obeying the law and staying on the proverbial straight and narrow path, and following his determined wife, John took all of three seconds to make a choice. It wasn't like they were stealing. They'd been specifically asked by the locker's owner to retrieve items. Move them, briefly. Ignoring a little voice reminding him the police were likely arresting the locker's owner for murder right now, John headed after Daphne.

He caught up at the top where she'd paused to look around, presumably for other people. She really was good at this cloak-and-dagger stuff.

Daggers are knives. Not a good analogy.

'Oh, well seeing as you're here, let's check that fire door.'

And with that, Daphne was off again.

The heavy fire door only took a bit of effort to open and Daphne stuck her head inside. 'Hello? Anyone here?'

At first there was silence and then a thud.

'Kenny? Anyone? It's just Daphne and John.'

But all was quiet again. Most likely it was the roof popping as the sun warmed it. Theirs did that at home sometimes. She waited for John – who seemed unusually slow today – and told him the coast was clear. He didn't look impressed about the whole thing and she didn't blame him. Poor Susan! First she had to deal with her ex-husband writing a fake review about her cooking. Then he died. And now she was accused of killing him.

Well, she didn't. I'm as certain as I was about Lisa Brooker having not killed her husband in Little Bridges last year. And look how that turned out.

The staff room was even fuller than last time, with several more boxes piled near the row of tall lockers.

'Do you know which is hers?' John was almost right behind now.

'Each one has a name at the top. Oh, dandelions and daffodils! This doesn't feel right, John.'

She swung around to face him, hand over her mouth.

'This is why I was reluctant, doll. We have no idea what's going on. What evidence the police have, because they must have enough to arrest her rather than simply question her.'

Stop making so much sense.

Daphne glanced at the locker and then back at John. 'I'm not sure how she had my number or why she phoned me rather than Belle or Heather. But Susan is taking a huge chance asking us to help her. For all she knows, we might simply call the police and tell them. And share the padlock's combination.'

'Even so...'

'Do *you* think she killed him?'

John shook his head.

'Are there gloves around? Anything at all.'

'I'll try the kitchen.'

Alone in the staff room, Daphne took a deep breath. She was running on pure adrenaline and needed to think this through. Inside this locker was Susan's knife roll, assuming she'd left it in there. And what else? She'd said to take it all. Was this the worst decision ever? What if Susan *was* a killer and Daphne was about to become an accessory after the fact?

'The place is in darkness but I found some. What's wrong?'

John held out thin latex gloves.

'Second-guessing myself.'

'We can justify it however we like, Daph, but this is a potential minefield.'

She took a couple of steps away and stared at the locker as if expecting it to provide answers to her dilemma.

'Susan sounded frustrated and worried. She's certain she's being set up and you know I can't abide people casting blame on an innocent party. In this case, it is probably the killer behind it. But the police are the ones with forensics and access to information we aren't privy to. If we touch anything in there it might actually go against Susan.'

There had to be some middle ground which would help her without putting themselves on the wrong side of the law.

'Okie dokie.' Daphne turned to John. 'Get your camera ready. I'll open the locker and you photograph the contents. Then we'll close it again. You know how much I respect the police force but Jeremy has already acted strangely on several occasions. What if he's behind Godfrey's death and is not only covering his tracks but also setting someone else up?'

'Just photos.' John found his phone. 'Everything will stay as we find it?'

'Yes, dear.'

After putting on the gloves, Daphne held the padlock and turned each number. 'Seven... oh, already on that. Three.' She peered at the numbers. 'John, just take a photo please. This isn't locked.'

He zoomed in.

'Done.'

With just the slightest of tugs, the padlock opened.

'I saw Susan spin this after putting her knives in earlier. But this was still on the combination, so has someone opened it already or did she just forget to lock it the last time she used it?' She slid the padlock off and put it on top of the closest box which, oddly, didn't look sealed.

'Be cautious with the door, doll. Just in case anything falls out.'

'I will be.'

The door squeaked a little as Daphne peered through the crack. It was too dark to see anything so she opened it wide then stood back. 'Do you want to take a series of photos?'

While John did so, she checked out the locker. There were two shelves above a hanging space. The latter held a couple of chef's whites, some aprons, and a clothes bag. One shelf had two chef's hats and the knife roll. The other held a small metal box with a key in its lock.

'Would you carefully move the clothes to one side so I can photograph the shoes?'

There were three pairs. Comfortable runners, a pair of steel-capped boots for the kitchen, and a pair of short rubber boots pushed toward the back and splashed with dried mud.

'Done.'

'While we're here, we should look at the knives.' Before John could say anything, Daphne picked up the roll, almost dropping it. 'Whew. I had no idea it would weigh so much. I might put them on the bench there.'

'I'm not sure we should open it.'

Daphne already had it on the long seat and undid a buckle. 'This is for photographic purposes only.' She unrolled the fabric, revealing half a dozen pouches with a variety of knives. 'Oh, these are stunning, love. I've seen that brand and they are not cheap. And is that an inscription?'

'Hang on a sec and I'll see how close I can zoom... yes. Each handle is engraved. It says "SG, the chef's kiss".' He took some images and then showed Daphne. 'Perhaps a gift?'

'I can't see Susan calling herself the chef's kiss. Maybe... what if Godfrey gave them to her? What if that was what he meant by *tell Susan... knife*. It could have been the last goodbye. Regret.

Didn't Belle say he hadn't wanted the divorce but she'd had enough of his wandering ways? But look, John, there's an empty pouch.'

The knives were in order of size and the space between a paring knife and small chef's knife logically would house something narrow and probably quite sharp.

'Belle might know what's missing. I imagine chefs have their own way of ordering knives.'

Daphne carefully re-rolled the set and buckled it, then put it back exactly where she'd found it. 'Should we open the metal box? She said to take everything out before the police get here.'

'What was that?' John interrupted her abruptly.

'What?'

John was still, listening. Behind him, the staff door moved ever so slightly.

'Someone's out there,' Daphne whispered.

She quietly closed the locker and reluctantly replaced the padlock, ensuring she left it on the combination. Everything had to be the way they'd found it. They went to the door and John pushed it open enough to see down the short hallway.

'The coast is clear.'

They quickly left the building through the fire door, which was wide open. It was only when they were a few metres away that Daphne stopped them both.

'That was closed when we arrived. I had to pull on the handle to open it.'

'The fire door? I mustn't have closed it properly when I stepped inside.' But he was frowning. 'I'm sure I did. And we heard someone.'

'And I thought I heard a thud before we went in.'

John took her arm. 'We are going home to Bluebell. I think we need to have a talk about all of this and see if we need to bring Eddie and Heather into what we've found, before whoever was in there with us gives them the wrong idea.'

I hadn't considered that. If we've been seen then we might as well have opened the metal box as well.

Daphne gazed around. 'The place feels deserted. You said the kitchen is in darkness and we know the front door was locked before. Arvin had somewhere to be. Heather and Belle might still be out doing wedding stuff. Let's pop back to the cellar door. See if Eddie is around.'

After a moment's hesitation, John nodded. 'Makes sense if we can see him, because I don't think we have his or Heather's phone numbers.'

Taking the ramp to the carpark, they cut through the old trees to the cellar door. The only person in there was the other man they'd seen earlier behind the counter with Arvin. He didn't know where Eddie was but wrote his number on a card.

Only the barrel hall was left and at first, Daphne thought it was empty. But Claude was pacing the stone floor, talking rapidly on his phone. Not wanting to interrupt, they decided against going in. But for the first time it occurred to Daphne that perhaps they hadn't factored in all the potential suspects.

Where had Claude been that fateful night?

TWENTY-TWO

Daphne's brain hurt from too many thoughts. Well, she knew her brain couldn't hurt as such but certainly overthinking wasn't a pleasant feeling. She still wished they'd at least looked inside that metal box. Or brought everything with them.

Instead of their earlier plans of John fishing and Daphne updating her notebook, both sat near the water's edge, each with a cup of tea. The trip home had been quiet other than Daphne sending a message to Arvin about Susan's phone call. His reply came fast.

> We're at the police station now.

No mention of who 'we' was but it was reassuring Susan wasn't dealing with this alone.

'What do you think we should do, love?' Daphne finally asked. 'I can't imagine how Belle is feeling right now.'

'We can phone her. See if there's anything we can do.'

He sounded as down and helpless as she felt.

'Hopefully Susan has a good lawyer. Oh dear, that sounds insensitive. But she didn't kill Godfrey, so maybe someone from his firm will help her.'

John opened his phone and began scrolling through the images he'd taken, Daphne looking over his shoulder.

'Unless there's something incriminating in the metal box, there's really nothing which stands out as being a problem. Maybe the muddy boots. And the missing knife,' Daphne said. 'Actually, it would be good to find out more about her knives and see if our theory pans out about them being a gift from Godfrey. If he was thinking about her in his last moments, then it backs up Belle's words about him not wanting the divorce.'

Putting the phone away, John gazed at her.

'What's behind that look? What are you thinking?'

'So much guesswork. We don't know for certain that Godfrey was stabbed but if he'd seen his attacker, or even just the weapon, well—'

'He'd have recognised Susan's knife! Oh, that does make sense. Yes, yes indeedy. Godfrey clearly said "tell Susan" and after trying to catch his breath, "knife". Not "Susan stabbed me with her knife" or even close. You are clever, love.'

At last there was a small smile on her husband's face. 'Do you think we can narrow down who had access to the knives that night?'

'And also had means and motive. The other thing which keeps puzzling me is how Godfrey ended up on that track. I keep wondering whether the whole food critic review thing was a joke gone wrong. That Godfrey was deliberately baiting Susan for some reason. He certainly seemed to be enjoying himself when she stormed out.'

'If it was, then that does put her back in the frame for his murder.' John's forehead creased in concentration. 'Pretty straightforward, I imagine, if you were a police officer investigating this. One horrible review. An ex-wife who happens to be the head chef. She confronts him and what might be a threat is made. Susan returned to the kitchen, picked up a knife, and waited for him to leave.'

'Except that he should have been with his dinner companions, all in the same car. How would she have known he had gone outside alone?'

'I'm trying to recall the sequence of events,' John said. 'His guests left first... oh wait, Jeremy stayed. So Warren and Aleesha rushed out without paying... actually, did they leave together? Then Godfrey. And I'm sure Kenny asked him for payment and was ignored. Then Kenny vanished before Jeremy left because Heather went to take care of the account. And Kenny only reappeared – from what I recall – after I called the ambulance.'

Daphne gasped. 'Surely Kenny isn't the killer?'

'Would there have been time to get a knife, run down to the path, find Godfrey and commit murder? For either of them?'

'I think I can go back to my notes now, thanks to your wonderful insights.'

At least Daphne was back in the right head space to be useful. Instead of worrying about things outside her control – such as how to magically get Susan released and all charges dropped – she could put her mind to the job of working out who really did murder Godfrey.

'By tonight if possible,' she muttered.

She collected what she needed for the task at hand and laid them on the table.

The notebook.

Pens in blue, black and red.

A ruler.

A scribble pad.

After pouring a glass of water she made herself comfortable and reread her notes so far. There were some points she'd forgotten and others which no longer applied. The latter she crossed out. The one thing which felt relevant, in fact highly relevant, was that Susan had done a deep clean of the kitchen the night of the murder, staying there until two in the morning. According to Belle.

Daphne wrote a few lines in the notebook, all speculation.

Who knew about the deep clean of the kitchen? Have they told the police during interviews, therefore making Susan look like she had something to hide? Why didn't she know her knife was missing until today? Is it really missing or just somewhere in the kitchen?

On her scribble pad, Daphne wrote a series of large questions marks and 'Godfrey's cause of death'. Without knowing if it *was* from a knife, this might be a wasted exercise.

She put her pen down and sipped her water.

Inside the cold walls of a police station not far away, a truly lovely woman was no doubt frightened and stressed about her future. Belle had said that Susan, along with Heather and Daphne, were like mothers to her. Daphne's gut was usually right and from the moment she'd laid eyes on Godfrey along that path, her gut said a knife or similar was involved.

Checking her earlier notes and memory as she went, Daphne wrote a line or two about each person who might have had a motive to murder, making sure to include where they were when the review was made public as well as around the time his body was discovered.

Susan: Confronted GG then ran to kitchen right after he left. Belle found her outside the building on her phone after GG died. **Q:** Was there time to get her knife, kill him, and return?

Jeremy: Left well after GG – as designated driver the others had to wait for him. On scene after everyone else. **Q1:** But how would he have got into the staff room or kitchen for knife? **Q2:** Why did it take so long for him to arrive on the scene of the crime?

Kenny: In restaurant when GG left. Then vanished rather than serve Jeremy. Came to scene of crime with John and did CPR. **Q1:** Where was he in between? **Q2:** Did he have access to knife?

Arvin: In restaurant when GG left. Went with Eddie to check

GG was leaving property. Back while Jeremy was still in restaurant and didn't leave again. **Q:** where was he when everyone else attended scene?

Eddie: Same as Arvin. No time to kill and physical limitations to go along path. **Q:** where was he when everyone else attended scene?

Warren: Left at same time as Aleesha? They arrived together at the scene of the crime.

Aleesha: Left after review posted but before GG left. Says she was in carpark waiting. Returned when Rhianna was meeting husband. Arrived with Warren just after John.

Lainie: Outside smoking when GG left. Was with Russell upset afterwards.

Belle: Walked Rhianna to meet husband after GG left and after Jeremy left. Aleesha returned to look for GG at the same time Belle was going. Belle was only away for a couple of minutes. She would have access to a knife but no time to kill.

> *Not that you ever would, darling.*

Daphne ran her eye over the notes. She'd only included those whom she'd personally seen come or go or John had told her about. And although Russell and Lainie had left the restaurant for a while, it seemed to be after Godfrey was found.

There were also the other serving staff and possibly cooks who might have left the building but without some way to verify their movements, it was speculation. With so many people who had the opportunity to follow Godfrey – possibly lure him along the track and fatally wound him – why was Susan the one arrested?

Focusing only on what she had written about Susan, Daphne expanded on the earlier conversation with John about what the police might see as incriminating evidence… or at least, behaviour suspicious enough to put all their eggs into her basket.

Godfrey had written a scathing food review which while not naming Susan as head chef, was still clearly directed at her. She confronted him in front of other people and replied to his question about whether she'd throw a knife at him with 'this time I won't miss'. Not only might it sound like a threat, but it implied a past attempt on his life. Less than half an hour later he was dead.

Had Susan immediately collected her knife and gone outside, she'd have seen Godfrey storm off a short time later. Or maybe she waited at the bottom of the stairs and somehow persuaded him to go into the dense bush. It wouldn't take long, Daphne imagined, to stab him and possibly hit him with a rock, before returning to the kitchen. More likely she'd gone to hide the knife elsewhere until she could be certain nobody would see her with it. What if she'd got blood on her clothing? Was that why there was a clothes bag in the locker? Freshly cleaned whites not yet hung out for use? Then she'd stayed in the kitchen for hours doing a deep clean, when it wasn't normally her job. Finally, which the police wouldn't know until they opened her locker, there were the muddy boots. It had rained that night.

'Oh, Susan, it isn't looking good for you,' Daphne sighed.

Yet there was much which didn't add up and was worth writing down:

- Why was Susan so upset to find a knife was missing from her roll?
- In the staff room she told me to tell the police what I'd seen and heard
- She thought nobody would believe her anyway
- By asking me to take everything from her locker she was trusting we wouldn't simply go to the police about it – and she knew the boots and knife roll were in there, let alone anything else
- She was convinced someone was setting her up

None of it offered any facts. No evidence, unless something in the locker could prove she wasn't anywhere near Godfrey after he left that night. But had Daphne and John removed anything, they might be accused of tampering with evidence and that wouldn't help Susan either.

Daphne stared at the notebook and scribble pad. If she couldn't prove Susan wasn't a killer, all she could do was come up with a good argument that another person *was*. Claude had to be brought into the situation.

This might take a while.

She picked up her pen.

Evening was closing in as John cleaned up after scaling and filleting the fish he'd caught. He'd stuck his head into Bluebell on his return. The table was covered with Daphne's 'tools of the trade' and she waved and went back to writing furiously. He wasn't about to disturb her while in sleuth mode, although he longed to talk about the events of the day.

While sitting lakeside with only the occasional curious duck for company, his body had relaxed but his mind couldn't settle. Logically, not taking the contents of the locker had been the correct decision, for several reasons. The despair in Susan's voice during their short phone call haunted him. He didn't believe for one minute she'd killed her ex-husband. Looking through the photos earlier, he was pleased they'd at least got those because if Susan was right about being set up, they might help.

'Ooh, that's a decent size fish, love. I brought you an icy cold beer.'

John quickly dried his hands and gladly took the open bottle from Daphne. She held up a glass of white wine and they tapped them together with a 'Cheers'.

The first sip was delightful and he took another, enjoying the taste and little bit of a lift.

He leaned over and kissed her cheek. 'Best wife ever.'

'Only wife ever. Remember I am quite knowledgeable about how to hide a body, dear. In case you ever considered wooing another.'

Thank goodness he hadn't taken another sip. It would have spurted out of his mouth for sure. She had a look of such innocence on her face and he wanted to gather her in his arms and deliver a proper kiss. But he smelled too fishy for that.

Pretending he didn't hear, John gestured to the fish. 'Tacos?'

She giggled.

'Now, why is that funny?'

'Because you are a smooth operator, John Jones. What if I go and prep the other ingredients and you do your magic with the fish?'

'Or, I could do everything while you sit and relax and enjoy your wine.'

Her expression changed and he knew her well enough to understand. Her stress levels were right up there, thanks to the abundance of empathy and love in her heart which currently was manifesting as worry.

'In fact, I'd love it if you sat here and talked me through your thoughts from the last couple of hours. If you feel up to it?' He pulled one of the chairs a bit closer to his cooking station and then a small table, which he placed beside the chair. 'All I need is a couple of minutes in Bluebell to gather my ingredients.'

For a moment she hesitated but then, with a long sigh, she sat. 'Thank you. As long as you don't need me to help?'

'You have already.' He lifted the beer then placed it on the table near her. 'Be right back.'

Inside Bluebell, John quickly collected what he wanted to make the tacos, and added the open bottle of wine and a second glass to the tray. Tonight they needed to step back and try to enjoy their time in the town. With a bit of luck, they could have a calm and happy evening.

TWENTY-THREE

Thank goodness for John.

The soft light of dusk enveloped Daphne. In the distance, magpies sang their evening song. And a mosquito buzzed around her head until it landed on her arm and she slapped it.

For some reason beyond her comprehension, that action made her cry.

Silly tears which dripped down her cheeks.

She let them.

Nobody was here to see. Not John... he didn't need more emotion and drama today. Not Belle whose big day might be ruined. And definitely not her darling friends in Rivers End. They were used to smiles and kind words. Not sorrow.

The past few days had tested her. Arriving here already missing home and wishing for the impossible, Daphne was overjoyed to have reunited with Annabelle. Beautiful Belle, who was as fierce and clever as she'd always been, despite having a father who allowed others to dictate his relationships, including with his daughter. And Arvin. He'd brought the love and happiness into Belle's life that she deserved. Heather was a guiding light, and then there was Susan. A mentor in the restaurant and a wonderful part of Belle's life.

How will Belle cope with all of this?

'Here we go... oh. Darling girl.'

Even as she looked away and brushed the tears from her cheeks, Daphne sensed John putting his tray down and kneeling at her side. His fingers cupped her cheeks as his thumbs wiped the tears.

'What a week we've had. Good and bad moments. I bet you feel exhausted.'

'I killed a mozzie.'

He chuckled.

'My brain is struggling with all the worries and woes.'

'Mine too, doll. Shall I feed us and you can talk a bit about what you've worked out?'

Not nearly enough, and time's running out.

John set about making his delicious tacos while Daphne ran through the breakdown of data about where people were the night of the murder.

'I feel that for Susan to be the culprit, she'd have needed to pick up a knife and immediately go to the bottom of the steps. It seems more logical someone lured Godfrey along the path rather than him just going with them for a chat.'

'Unless she was counting on his reluctance for the divorce to put him off guard?'

'Hmm. Maybe. But the fact remains that as far as we know, none of the other cooks or servers noticed her leaving. And Kenny went to the kitchen only a minute or two after Godfrey left.'

Holding up tongs, John gave her a thoughtful look. 'Do we know he was in the kitchen?'

'Actually, no.' She sighed. 'Sometimes I wish I was a proper detective and had the authority to question people, because I have so many questions.'

'One thing playing on my mind is probably not helpful.'

'Everything is helpful, love. Goodness me, those are smelling nice!'

'New taco mix with extra paprika for a bit more smokiness.' He turned down the heat on the small burner. 'I wonder if the killer is someone who wasn't in the restaurant at all.'

'A complete stranger? Well that would change things. Or... whoever is behind those letters.' Daphne almost dropped her wine glass in her hurry to stand. 'Someone who wants Crystal Springs sold so badly they threaten and attack people, might be out of patience. What could be worse for a business than a murder on the grounds?'

'It had an immediate effect, doll. Didn't Susan say about half their restaurant bookings cancelled the next day?'

'And a third of the wedding guests.'

'Where are you going?'

'To get my phone.'

It only took a minute to collect her phone and return. John was filling the plates and her tummy rumbled. 'I have the phone number of Constable Woodcroft, so thought I'd alert her about the letters... oh. I can't, can I?'

'Not without putting Eddie and Heather in the spotlight. They don't know we've seen the letters, so having the police suddenly asking might make things quite awkward for Arvin and Belle.'

'Bother.' Daphne sank back in her seat. 'In that case we need to speak to Arvin and explain the importance of coming clean with his parents. Do you think I should phone him now?'

'I think we should eat first. And shall I top up your wine?'

Dinner was yummy and helped settle Daphne's racing thoughts. Over the meal the conversation steered away from the current troubles, instead talking about Rivers End and how much they both looked forward to being home.

'I thought we might leave earlier than planned, doll.' John collected both plates. 'Sunday morning, if that suits you?'

'We won't have any real reason to stay after the wedding. Belle will be on her honeymoon. And we're not going to be much help here. I guess it isn't our problem to solve.'

Except Daphne had pages of her thoughts written down and a couple of sketches. One was a rough floorplan of the restaurant, complete with where people had sat that night. The other was of the grounds, including the lake, cellar door and barrel room. She'd estimated where she'd found Godfrey and marked that as well.

'Circling back to an earlier conversation, love...' Daphne followed John into Bluebell, carrying the pans he'd cooked with. 'What do you think about Claude as a potential suspect?'

'He's an interesting character, certainly. Maybe we should take a look at him. I mean, his background, which I seem to recall is on the Crystal Springs website.'

'It is a bit of a puzzle. The people and how they all fit. Russell and Claude, for example. Remember how Claude told Belle to ask her father why he is unhappy? And then Russell did everything other than provide a straight answer.'

'I know that you overheard part of his and Belle's conversation, but afterwards the two of you wandered around the lake and there was a lot of quiet talking going on.'

'Oh goodness, yes. Completely forgot to update you. Russell kept going on about how it was Arvin's time to be head winemaker and how well Belle had done for herself. Afterwards, Belle told me her grandmother had a meltdown when she left school so early and told Russell to send Belle away.'

'Her own grandchild?'

'Yup. Now, people have told me she loved Belle but my gut tells me the woman loved being in charge even more. She'd wanted Belle to become a doctor or a lawyer, not a lowly cook, as she put it. So my theory is that in a twisted way, Russell sees Belle's marriage as a type of validation. If her new husband becomes the head winemaker at a prestigious winery, then she has more status.'

John frowned as he began to wash up while Daphne put cold items into the fridge. 'If Russell's mother had such influence over him then maybe he thinks a similar way. Status, money, power before family.'

'Which makes me wonder if he has encouraged Claude to move elsewhere.'

'Yet, it isn't quite adding up.' John held a dish brush aloft, bubbles dripping to the water below. 'Why tell Belle to ask Russell what's wrong rather than simply tell her himself? No, there's more to it.'

'But what? I'll get the laptop up and running as soon as we're done here.'

'Go ahead. This is almost finished.'

Daphne quickly made space on the table and got the laptop started. By the time John sat, she was typing in the website of the winery. 'I remember us taking a look a while ago but don't recall too much other than thinking how pretty the grounds are.'

'There's a page for the key staff.'

The page loaded with a black and white photo at the top. Pictured were half a dozen people standing around a huge barrel.

'Oh, look at this, love. This is Eddie's grandparents. What a lovely legacy.'

'A true family business. And some dreadful person has made it their concern to damage its reputation and threaten hard-working people.'

'Quite possibly even more than threaten, John. The letter I saw at the shop which had closed up? It was positively gleeful about accomplishing the goal of ruining a small business and at the expense of poor Tori; because the way it was worded, I am certain they ran her off the road. And that has to be a connection to Eddie's accident and the letters. We have to talk to them about it!'

Putting an arm around her shoulders, John held her against him. 'We will. There's too much at stake to stand by and see Belle's family-to-be suffer more than they already have.'

She leaned her head against him for a moment, letting the warmth of his embrace calm her spirit. The feelings were bubbling beneath the surface all the time right now but she'd not expected to get so worked up.

John took over the mouse and scrolled slowly down the page, which was a series of photos with a brief description.

'Eddie, general manager. And a bit about the family traditions. Heather, past head chef and now semi-retired. Ah, here we go. Claude, head winemaker for eighteen years. Responsible for the following gold and silver medal-winning vintages... and there's an impressive list. Educated in winemaking in France before migrating to Australia. And that's it.'

'What about Susan?' Daphne straightened.

'Not here. Neither is Belle. Perhaps they kept it to the winery rather than the restaurant.'

Headlights from an approaching vehicle shone through the window and a car pulled up close to Bluebell. John immediately went to the door with Daphne close behind.

'Oh, it's Heather.'

'Is Eddie with her? Or Belle?'

The interior light came on as Heather climbed out. She was alone.

'Thank goodness you are both here.' Heather closed the door and hurried over. 'Can we have a quick chat?'

'Of course. Please come in.'

Daphne grabbed the laptop off the table, closing it and popping it onto a benchtop. How strange would it appear if Heather saw them checking out the staff at the winery.

'Come and sit, dear. We were about to make a pot of tea. Or coffee if you prefer?'

Heather clutched a soft briefcase against her chest. Her eyes were red-rimmed and when John shut the door, she visibly jumped.

'I can't do this alone any longer. Belle told me you've solved criminal cases and I think... well, I *know*, that I need help. Desperately.' She gazed at Daphne. 'My entire world is at risk of collapsing and some of it is my own doing. Susan is in awful trouble and I think I've made a terrible mistake.'

TWENTY-FOUR

With a nice pot of tea brewing and a plate of chocolate biscuits served, they gathered at the table. Heather took one side, putting the briefcase beside her on the seat and unzipping it but not revealing the contents.

'We were just talking about you. Your winery and the family and staff.' Daphne offered Heather and then John a biscuit. 'What we are struggling with is understanding some of the connections people have to each other. Like Russell and Claude.'

'Well, they're friendly enough and Claude is a good man. Russell is a...' Heather stopped herself.

'A what, dear?'

'I can't. He's Belle's father and I'd never hurt her by speaking my mind about that man.'

'Only for our ears and I doubt there's much you can say that I haven't thought.' Daphne was proud of how she kept her voice calm. 'We're just trying to understand.'

John poured the tea and passed everyone a cup, which let Heather take a moment to think. Eventually she nodded.

'All of my life I've strived to be kind and caring. I don't enjoy conflict and hate seeing anyone or anything suffer.'

No wonder I like you so much. We're kindred spirits.

'But Russell sometimes makes me want to shake him. He has a weak personality and is easily led astray. He was seeing someone else when he met Belle's mother. He was on a working holiday in the west of the state. Went back to visit her a few times and the poor woman knew nothing about his two-timing until she fell pregnant and he turned his back on her. You see, his mother wanted him to marry the first woman and made such a fuss that he fell into line. He regrets it now. Loves Belle to bits but he lets people walk over him. Like now with Lainie.' Heather grimaced. 'Everything with Lainie is about ambition, just like his mother was, which I feel is creating some tension with her and Russell.'

Heather reached into her briefcase. 'I have to show you these. I really don't know what to do because of the mess I've made.'

She took out a folder and placed it on the table.

'You will think I am the worst person but I was just trying to help.'

The folder contained half a dozen sheets of paper, each one inside a plastic sleeve. Even as Heather pushed them across the table, Daphne's heart had sunk. It was more of the letters. She heard John's swift intake of breath.

'Before you read them I need to tell you that Eddie and I have been receiving similar letters for a long time.'

'May we?' John asked with a quick smile.

'I have to warn you, these contain threats.'

Each letter was typed in the same typeface as those Daphne had previously seen. The tone was increasingly nasty, with the last one particularly unpleasant.

You think Im joking about this?

Last chance.

Quit. Get everyone to quit. Tell people how badly you were treated there. Or else find another way to destroy them.

If you dont youll live to regret it.

'The syntax and dreadful grammar is the same as the others, love.' Daphne hadn't meant to say that and darted a look at Heather.

'The others? Do you mean our letters? It was Arvin, wasn't it?'

Shuffling in her seat Daphne nodded. 'Sorry. Yes. Well, Belle really. She is so worried about you both and said the police can't do anything.'

'And that's the thing, Daphne. If the police see these letters and we show them ours again then perhaps they'll have more to go on. But I don't think I can take them to the police. Not without getting some legal advice first.'

'Do you mind if I take some photos of these?' John asked.

'Go ahead.'

'I am a bit confused, dear. Each of the letters mentions quitting a job and telling people about being badly treated. The other ones, which Arvin showed us, were nasty attacks on Eddie and mentioned you and Arvin in one. And owners of a business don't quit. They sell.'

'Except these aren't meant for Eddie or me and that's where my problem lies.' Heather drew in a long breath, her colour high. 'These were sent to Susan. It's like the sender was forcing her to resign and do damage to our reputation as her employers. Yet another attempt to make us leave our home.'

John put down his phone. 'Susan? Then the police need to see these.'

'What if it makes things worse?' Panic widened Heather's eyes. 'What if they think she killed Godfrey because the letter suggested she should find another way to destroy us? Rather than quit, what if they think she killed Godfrey to bring bad publicity to our winery?'

Reaching out her hand, Daphne squeezed Heather's arm. 'We probably need to trust the police on this. I'd say it's more likely Godfrey was killed in order to frame Susan because she *didn't* do what the sender demanded. She was certain she was being set up.'

'Then I've made things harder... for my... family.'

The last words came out as sobs and John patted her on the shoulder until she regained her composure. She thankfully accepted a tissue from Daphne and blew her nose then took another sip of tea.

'After Susan was arrested, the police came to the restaurant. They searched the kitchen and staff room and made a dreadful mess. Some of the wedding decorations are damaged. Then they opened all the lockers.'

Oh... the metal box. I should have checked it.

'They found something inside Susan's locker which wasn't there before.'

'Before?'

Heather nodded. 'And I don't know how because I locked the padlock.'

John looked as confused as Daphne felt. 'I feel we're missing some of the story, Heather.'

'The reason I'm reluctant to go to the police is that I took it upon myself to move some of Susan's belongings to a safe place. She'd left me a message on my phone saying the police were coming and she couldn't lose her knives because it was the only gift from Godfrey she'd kept. When I arrived – which took a little while as I was driving home when she messaged me – it was still full. I took the knives and something made me grab the metal box and some other items as well.'

'So what was the extra thing the police found?'

'This is the worst part because it might be the thing which incriminates Susan.' Heather's voice dropped to a whisper. 'They found an old typewriter.'

The car's headlights illuminated the Crystal Springs Winery sign as they followed Heather's car through the gates. For the first time since they'd been visiting, the gates had been closed and only swung open when Heather tapped in a code.

After a joint decision to help clean up the mess left by the police, Daphne hadn't said a word since they'd left Bluebell and for once, John couldn't gauge her mood. Whether it was the shock of Heather's news or her mind working overtime to process all the information, she'd kept her own counsel so far. But when they turned into the carpark, she suddenly straightened.

'It has to be to do with the permit.'

'Permit?'

'The planning approval for the wine retreat. I mean, I need to confirm the timing of it all but now there are three different recipients of those letters, with two being closely tied to here... if only there were more details about the one sent to Tori's employer.'

'Ask Belle.'

'Belle is getting married tomorrow but instead of relaxing tonight, she's coping with more than any young bride should. I'd rather not add to her burdens by worrying her with this, love. All we can hope is that common sense prevails at the police station and Susan is released in time for the ceremony.'

John parked beside Heather's car and Daphne was out before he'd turned off the motor. She was talking to Heather by the time he'd locked the car.

'Do you recall if the police took copies of the letters you and Eddie received?'

'No. Not even a statement.'

'And who else might know about Susan's letters?'

Ooh... I see where you're going, you clever cookie.

Heather frowned. 'Hmm. I only know because I cleared out her locker. And we're close. She doesn't have a significant other and like so many head chefs, tends to socialise little other than with staff.'

'Kenny, maybe?'

'I doubt it. He keeps to himself a lot. And I'm certain if she'd told Belle that, we'd also know. Not that I knew she'd been showing you our letters.' Heather's smile softened the words. 'She has a good heart, that one, and always looks out for others. But why do you ask?'

'Where have you stashed Susan's things from her locker?'

Now, Heather grinned. 'I know the good hiding places.'

'In that case, maybe put those letters with them? Just for the moment, until you can get legal advice.'

After reaching into her car for the briefcase, Heather again held it against herself. 'You'd better go up to the restaurant rather than see me commit more crimes. I'll be there in a few minutes.' She suddenly lowered the briefcase and hugged Daphne. 'Thank you for helping me. For helping us all. Now, off you go.'

Daphne was clearly reluctant but let John take her hand and they climbed the steps, neither looking back.

'Are you thinking what I am?' she asked.

'With no letters, the typewriter isn't any kind of evidence.'

'We'll make a sleuth of you yet. Whoever is behind all of these crimes... the letters, Eddie and Tori being run off the road, Godfrey's murder... they've planted what they believe is solid evidence to incriminate Susan and potentially ruin Crystal Springs from the scandal.'

'Still a stretch, doll. Whoever's behind this expected the letters to Susan to be found, and probably is relying on Eddie and Heather coming forward again with their letters.'

They reached the top and stopped. The restaurant was lit up as though full for the night, yet the fact the gates were closed said otherwise.

'There's two people. Possibly more. And as much as I don't want to believe it, one of them works here. Either in the restaurant or in the winery, and knows the fire door is generally left unlocked during the day... we know someone was around when we were here earlier. My guess is that they aren't the mastermind but more of an assistant. We need to keep our wits about us.'

'Auntie Daph!'

Belle was weeping as she ran toward them.

It was time to find the culprit. Nobody was hurting Belle any more on John's watch.

Daphne almost burst into tears seeing the destruction in the staff room. Boxes ripped open, contents strewn across the floor, decorations crushed or torn. Every locker was wide open and Susan's was covered with fingerprint dust.

'Is all this bad stuff happening to stop the wedding?' Belle had stopped crying but her eyes were puffy and her tone was flat. 'Getting Susan arrested. Ruining our decorations. But even if someone hates me, why kill Godfrey?'

'Babe, no, it isn't about you. Or me.' Arvin had a row of undamaged boxes and was sorting items into them. 'Nobody could ever hate you, anyway.'

Arvin held out his hand to Belle and she stepped over a box of squashed candles to reach him.

'It feels personal.'

'It is personal, babe, because you love Mum and Dad and the property and everyone who works here.'

'And you.'

His smile was a bit sad. 'I love you too, and I promise our wedding is going to be beautiful.' He gathered her in his arms and held her close.

'There's too much to do now.' Her voice was a bit muffled. 'Without Susan, how will this work?'

'We can help,' John said. 'Not that we're cooks, but I know how to peel potatoes.'

That made Belle smile as she stepped back from Arvin. 'You and Auntie are meant to be enjoying the reception, not working behind the scenes.'

'What was the original plan, dear? For setting up and cooking and so on?'

'All the prep was being done tonight. Susan, Heather, me, and if any other cooks wanted some extra money we were happy for them to come and help. Arvin and Eddie were going to get started on moving tables with Kenny and Mike so that in the morning the decorations could be finished.' Her face fell. 'But without Susan...'

'Without Susan we can still pull this together, Belle,' Daphne said.

John nodded. 'Would it be best to remove anything too damaged to use first and then see what can be salvaged? And I'm pretty handy when it comes to fixing things.' He found a roll of large thick plastic bags. 'Happy for me to use my judgement?'

'We didn't expect you to come and help, Uncle John. But thank you, yes.'

As they all got to work, Daphne's mind should have been on the job at hand yet her thoughts raced and collided. Who was behind the letters and everything that came with them? There were plenty of suspects and the evidence was mounting against Susan. But was she a killer?

TWENTY-FIVE

By the time Heather arrived, with Eddie at her side, most of the staff-room carnage was cleared away, leaving space for them both to come in. Followed in by Claude. Arvin visibly stiffened when their eyes met and then Claude held his arms wide and hugged the younger man.

Belle's eyes glistened and when Claude released Arvin, she mouthed, 'Thank you.'

'I want to help. Put me to work please.'

'What if some of us take a look at the restaurant and make a plan from there?' Eddie was already out of the door. 'Anybody who feels like lifting and possibly doing some repair work to decorations come this way.'

John kissed Daphne on his way past. He had a gleam in his eyes. Action was always the best approach under pressure. Claude and Arvin followed.

Daphne grinned at Belle and Heather. 'Who is up for some meal prep?'

'Men to the grunt work and women to the cooking?' Heather smiled. 'At least the kitchen is one of my happy places. Belle, go pop on all the lights and we'll be right behind you.'

Waiting until Belle was gone, and even checking through the doorway, Heather then quietly closed the door.

'Unless the police have x-ray vision and are willing to get their feet very wet, they won't locate the contents of Susan's locker. One of the benefits of living here for decades is knowing what is safe to climb into or not.'

Surely not in the lake?

'I'm guessing you don't want to share the location?'

'Not right now, which is for your protection. I had a phone call from our lawyer, who is at the police station now. He's managed to have the fingerprinting fast-tracked, with particular interest in those from the typewriter.'

'That's good news but even fast-tracked they can take days.'

'Yes, except they've gone to a private forensics company that the police already use sometimes so it might be as early as tomorrow. We told our lawyer we have absolute faith in Susan, so he's highly motivated. I've also asked for a meeting with him early tomorrow and will explain what I've done at that point.'

Daphne took Heather's hands and squeezed them. 'You were just doing what you thought was right. And Susan is your employee so I'd imagine there's an argument to be made that you simply stored some of her possessions until she could advise what to do with them. Were you asked if you'd touched them?'

'No. Actually, Jeremy was just intent on making as much mess as he could.' Heather gave Daphne a quick hug. 'We'd better catch up with Belle.'

They stepped out of the staff room but Daphne hesitated in the hallway. 'I'm still trying to understand the relationships here, Heather. The night Godfrey died, Jeremy was the last person sitting at his table and said something about not knowing if Godfrey was joking with the review or being serious. It seems they were close friends, so should Jeremy even be investigating this?'

Heather's eyes reflected Daphne's concerns. 'Probably not. But Jeremy is quite assertive. He likes to get his way. And I prefer to avoid him where possible because of Kenny. Although Kenny has never told me why he's afraid of Jeremy, it's clear he is and that it goes all the way back to when they worked together up north.'

'Have I been tricked into doing all this work on my own?' Belle's head appeared through the 'in' door of the kitchen. 'How about some actual assistance in here?'

Eddie had a floorplan of the wedding reception and directed the other men to carry and adjust tables until he was satisfied. Arvin had no issues picking up the smaller tables on his own while John and Claude collaborated.

'Actually, remove the last two please. Had another cancellation, so this is turning into a much smaller reception than planned. And then the chairs go around the outside.'

'More intimate receptions are nice, though,' John said. 'And this configuration allows everyone to see each other.'

A large U was formed, with the bridal party at the end and a row at right angles from either side.

'Belle likes the idea of servers being able to access the tables from the middle rather than reaching over the guests. Now that we're down to about fifty, this definitely feels more personal.'

'Right, before we pretty up the tables, let's see how bad the damage is.'

There was a flat trolley in a storeroom which Arvin and John loaded with boxes from the staff room. While they returned for a second load, Claude was emptying the contents onto one row of tables with Eddie helping to separate items. As they went past the kitchen, peals of laughter drifted out and Arvin stopped to peer through the small window in the door.

'They look happy. I think Daphne being here makes all the difference.'

'She loves Belle. Deeply loves her.'

'We were talking and thought we might come to Rivers End soon. Our honeymoon is only a week on a riverboat because the winery is still busy but we're going to sneak away in early winter. If you don't mind?'

'Mind? We'd be thrilled. We have a spare bedroom or else can arrange a lovely suite in Palmerston House, which is an historic bed and breakfast just a short walk away.'

Wait until I tell Daphne. This will keep her smiling for ages.

After the contents of the second trolley were sorted Eddie began reading off a long list. 'Let me know numbers of what isn't broken. Start with the paper lanterns.'

The results were mixed.

'I'm going to send the police department an invoice for all of the damage. All it would have taken was a little care.' Eddie rubbed his eyes. 'In some ways having fewer guests is a blessing in disguise.'

'Fewer tables to decorate,' John said. 'Is there a picture or diagram of what you want?'

'Yes. But that can be finished in the morning. The flowers don't arrive until ten and I'm confident Arvin and I can get this done in time.'

Eddie looked exhausted. So did Arvin, who pulled out a chair and sat.

'I'll keep working on it. Go and sleep, both of you.' Claude held his hand out for the diagram. 'You have enough to do tomorrow.'

'Count me in.' John checked his watch. 'Almost ten. I reckon we'll get this a long way by midnight. And I can't leave until Daph's finished.'

'It feels wrong to leave this all to you both.' Eddie wheeled around the table. 'Once upon a time I'd easily pull an all-nighter.'

He stopped near Claude, who dropped a hand onto his shoulder. 'Once upon a time you hadn't almost lost your life, Eddie. It takes time to rebuild your strength. Rebuild your business.'

'Which I couldn't have done without my family and without you, mate.'

'We need to talk. Next week.'

Eddie's face dropped but he nodded. 'Whenever you're ready.'

Surely you're not really leaving the winery? The respect you share is obvious.

Arvin pushed himself to his feet. 'I'll walk you home, Dad. But I'm coming back to help for a bit. And then to make sure Belle and Mum get home safely.'

Claude let them out of the front door, locking it and turning to John with a wry smile. 'Shall we?'

What an absolute treat it was working alongside Belle and Heather in a professional kitchen. It didn't matter that Daphne's feet ached from standing still for so long or her fingers were almost numb thanks to peeling and rinsing a mountain of vegetables. Just watching and listening was enough.

Belle had prepped the ingredients for the wedding dessert over the lunch service, in between other jobs, and was now in the creating stages.

'They need to be in the fridge overnight. I was going to do this earlier, then the police came.' She grimaced. 'So much has been disrupted that I honestly thought Arvin and I would need to delay the wedding.'

'Not if we can all help it,' Heather said. 'At the rate we're making progress we'll have almost everything ready for the line cooks. And if Susan isn't here, well I'll step in.'

'Heather, no! You have to be at the wedding. And the reception. Every minute of it!'

'I'm not missing that for anything, honey. I've thought it through and can have my hair and makeup done first then be in here as needed. The ceremony isn't until five, which is heaps of time. Then if I have to pop in here a few times during the reception I can.'

'What's the dessert?' Time to change the subject before Belle upset herself. 'It smells divine.'

Belle held up a martini glass. 'Tiramisu. It will be turned into towers of glasses with a choice of classic ingredients or lemon... and the lemons are grown here. Which reminds me, I haven't even shown you and Uncle John the vegetable gardens and orchard. Nor introduced you to the horses and donkeys. Will you please promise to come back and stay soon?'

As long as there's no more murders or arrests!

'We'd love to.'

'Speaking of lemons, do you want a few more over there, Belle?' Heather had gathered a bowlful. 'Or I can make garnishes?'

'Garnishes tomorrow is best. Have you seen Susan's knife roll?'

Heather's eyes widened. 'Um... why do you need it?'

Uh-oh. This might get messy.

'I don't. But it wasn't in the locker when the police opened it. Last time I saw it open she had shoes and clothes and stuff and it's where she locked the knives after every service.' Belle brushed hair from her eyes with the back of a hand. 'Those knives were a wedding gift from Godfrey and despite their differences, she treasures them. If you don't know then whoever left the typewriter must have taken the knives.'

Heather put down the lemons then picked up the bowl again. She seemed lost for words. The silence dragged.

'I meant to ask you, Belle... another visit, would you help me with some foolproof recipes for cookies? It appears mine weren't really all that nice.'

Belle's mouth opened and then she burst into laughter.

'Perhaps laughing isn't the right response, honey?' Heather looked confused.

Daphne couldn't keep a straight face. 'You know, you of all people should have told me the cookies I made almost daily were dreadful.'

'They weren't dreadful. Just not great.' Belle's eyes were amused. 'Of course I'll help you, but Auntie, what made those cookies special was not how they tasted, but how they made me feel. Loved. Always loved.'

. . .

The kitchen was in darkness and the small group gathered in the restaurant. It was a bit after midnight and more than time to get some sleep.

Belle wandered around the tables with soft exclamations of delight and Heather was beaming.

'This is so beautiful, love. You are all so clever.'

'We made a good team.'

The tables were set simply but with style. White tablecloths and serviettes, dark green placemats and table runners, other than the bridal party's which were a rich burgundy. Tall candle holders and fat vases. At one end was signage ready to hang tomorrow.

'Thank you. Thank you all for tonight.'

'No tears, Belle. I forbid it.' Daphne forced a smile to stop her own eyes misting again. 'John and I will drop you home for at least a few hours' sleep, so say goodnight to your groom.'

Heather and Claude double-checked that the front door was locked and then, turning lights off as they went, everyone exited through the fire door. There was a pile of cut-up boxes and bags of the damaged decorations outside and Claude picked up the bags. 'My car is near the barrel hall so I'll drop these into the bin on the way.'

'And I'll take the cardboard back inside to the storage room so we can pack up the decorations tomorrow night.' Arvin lifted an armful. 'I'll lock up. And thank you, every one of you.'

'I was wrong about your wedding,' Claude said. He glanced at Belle and then Arvin. 'Regardless of the turmoil and confusion of recent times, you will have a happy day. How could you not, surrounded by so many people who love you?' Turning on his heel, he was out of sight in a moment.

'Now we just need Susan back.' Belle spoke softly. 'It feels wrong to go ahead without her. She's innocent and somehow, we have to find a way to prove it.'

TWENTY-SIX

'You'll need to direct me to your home, Belle,' John said.

They'd just turned out of the driveway and the gates slowly closed behind them.

'Keep going along here for a while. And watch for kangaroos as they tend to be out and about this late. Just after the Benalla sign there's a left turn.'

Daphne turned in her seat to better see Belle. 'What you said about Susan earlier? Heather told me their lawyer is working hard behind the scenes. He's apparently challenged a few points of the arrest and has managed to fast-track the fingerprints from the typewriter. There'll be nothing of Susan, of course, and that might help.'

'Don't criminals wipe things down?'

'You'd be surprised how often people don't, even though we see it on so many television shows.'

The car braked and Daphne glanced forward in time to see a couple of large kangaroos bound across the road.

'Not wrong about the wildlife, Belle,' John said.

'That's why whoever ran Eddie off the road got away with it,' Belle said. Her voice was bitter, even angry. 'It happened just a bit further along when he was heading home after a council meeting, around a tight bend. I've driven with him a lot and Eddie is a careful driver. Well used to the roos and wombats and conditions. But that night, all he remembers is full beam headlights filling his rear vision mirrors before he woke up in hospital.'

'My goodness. So someone came up behind him, blinding him?'

'Except there's no proof. The police were thorough with their crash scene investigation but Jeremy said it was most likely Eddie braked hard to avoid hitting something and lost control.'

Jeremy again. Does he take over everything?

'Take this left, Uncle John. The speed limit drops here and in two blocks, take a right. It's a dead end road and Dad's house is at the end.'

As they passed a driveway, Belle pointed. 'Tori lives there with her parents and sisters.'

'How is she doing?'

'Still in a lot of pain. One of our friends is going to live stream the wedding to her tomorrow and I've told her to expect a meal delivered around the time of the reception. No way is she missing out on more than necessary.'

'How thoughtful,' John said.

He slowed to turn a corner.

'I don't wish to pry, dear, but Tori's accident? You mentioned she came off her motorcycle.'

'More that someone tailgated her and when she slowed to go around a curve their bumper hit the back of the bike and threw her into a ditch. It was between her place and the winery and she was going home after we'd had dinner to discuss the wedding. Rhianna was following a few minutes behind and thank goodness, because nobody had stopped to help.'

'Is this the right house?'

'Yes, just pull up here and I'll hop out.'

'Before you go... did the police find the culprit? Hit and run is a serious crime.'

'Not yet. Tori only saw it was a big ute of some kind and there was apparently no transfer of paint or whatever to her motorcycle. I'm just happy she's alive.' Belle opened the door. 'I can't thank you both enough for tonight and I'm going to go before I cry because I'm so tired and happy and really sad about Susan.'

'It was a pleasure, Belle. Try to sleep.' John wound down his window as she climbed out. 'We love you very much.'

'Love you, too!'

Belle closed her door and sprinted away to an imposing iron gate between brick pillars. On top of each was a concrete lion's head and there was a polished brass plate on one pillar with the name BOYD ESTATE. She pushed one of the gates until it gave and slipped through.

'We'll sit here for a moment, doll.' He turned off the motor and headlights. 'I know we can't see her but look at the lights coming on and then off again up the driveway. Motion sensor lights.'

'I can just see the roof of the house but it's quite a long way back. It looks huge, the property, not that we can tell too much in the dark. You have to wonder what Belle's life would have been like, and perhaps her mum's, had Russell done the right thing from the beginning.'

John's hand found Daphne's. 'Except she wouldn't be the Belle we know and love if he had. And she wouldn't have come into our lives and *that* I wouldn't swap for anything.'

You are so wise.

A text arrived on Daphne's phone and she read it aloud. 'Safely home. Thanks for the lift.'

'She must have known we'd wait for her to go inside. Just like we used to sit up on the occasional times she was out with a group of her friends. Now she's safe and sound, I can hear Bluebell calling.'

There was only one thing Daphne had to do before officiating the wedding. Finding the missing contents from Susan's locker was all that mattered and she couldn't stop searching until she did. The identity of the killer was among her possessions and even though Heather had hidden everything to protect Susan, the lawyer said time was running out.

She'd already searched around the lake, accidentally knocking over many of the chairs with their pretty bows.

Rowing one of the boats out to the middle turned into a nightmare when big waves pushed it into the reeds.

Yet now her feet were wet. Wasn't that what Heather had said? The police would need x-ray vision and to get their feet wet finding her hiding spot.

Daphne climbed up the ladder to the top of the highest wine vat. This had to be it. She was above the clouds, looking down at the world. People were waving. And John was calling. Calling loudly... 'Daph! Daphne!'

She jolted awake to the delectable aroma of coffee and for a moment lay with her eyes still closed, giving her heart a chance to slow its beat.

What a silly dream. Yet dreams often held answers thanks to the subconscious puzzling away in the background. Once she was out of bed, this big day would really begin and she wasn't quite ready.

Sometimes this adulting business gets a bit hard to do every day.

Weddings were her favourite thing in the world. Apart from being with John. And walking along the beach in Rivers End on a windy day.

But all the crime? Oh how she'd love for it to go away. People's hearts needed mending, not breaking. Happy days shouldn't be tarnished with the wrongdoings of others. And of everyone, it mattered that Belle's day was perfect.

Except it won't be. Even if Susan is released.

Perhaps if the true killer was caught? Daphne wasn't at all confident there was time for it to happen. Nor convinced anyone was looking because too much evidence pointed at poor Susan. It was as though the killer had orchestrated the time and place of Godfrey's murder in order to ruin the wedding.

She opened her eyes.

Crystal Springs was already a much-loved and popular wedding destination with its beautiful grounds and exceptional facilities. Hadn't Arvin mentioned that the new wine lovers' retreat was expected to increase revenue by some large figure? Which would make the winery even more valuable? But if some-one's wedding was a disaster – and surely having a murder on the premises qualified – then word would get around. The reputation of the place might be damaged beyond repair, leaving the Kingsley family to rebuild yet again. Maybe one time too many. It felt like a vendetta, but coming from whom and why?

Throwing off the covers, Daphne almost jumped out of bed, just as John popped his head in.

'Ah, you are awake. I'm making your favourite: chilli scrambled eggs.'

'Sounds wonderful, love. Care to pour some coffee and I'll throw on some clothes.'

He'd done more than pour coffee when she slid behind the table. Two plates with toast and eggs as well as orange juice kept them both busy for a few minutes and gave her a bit more time to get her thoughts in some kind of order.

'That was delicious, John, thank you. How long have you been up?'

'A little while. Went for a walk and took some photos.'

'I had the strangest dream about looking for the contents of Susan's locker because the lawyer said she was running out of time. I was looking all over the place, including the lake, and then I climbed up the side of a wine vat. All I could think about was Heather saying anyone searching would need x-ray vision and wet feet.'

'During the night you sat bolt upright and said, "Boots, muddy boots", then lay down and pulled half the blankets off me.'

'I did not steal the blankets.'

'You did. More coffee?'

'Please. Muddy boots. Well, I don't remember dreaming about those but it ties in with the one I do recall.'

'You're stressing about this, doll. I can see it in your eyes. How can I help?'

A massage? Magically solve the case?

Both sounded good.

'Photos... would you let me take a look at the ones you took of the locker?'

John swapped fresh coffee for the finished breakfast plates. 'I've uploaded them to the laptop, if you'd like me to collect it?'

'You are so thoughtful; yes, please. What would I do without you?'

The laptop fetched, John and Daphne sat together and opened the photos. 'Ooh, there's lots here from this trip, love.'

'I've put a fair few onto our blog already. Once we have some wedding photos, we can include those as well and add the ones you like most onto your website.'

Bluebell's Blessings was the name of the blog which John had started when they first began travelling. He'd filled it with snippets of their different journeys: maps, photos, and recommendations for places they'd visited.

'How many followers are there now?'

'Would you believe there's more than a thousand?' John sounded proud. 'Seems people are interested in our adventures.'

If only they knew some of the behind-the-scenes events.

John clicked on a folder containing a few dozen images and enlarged the first. 'I've included the photos you took when you found Godfrey Goffin. And others which I thought might be of use, although I never know what that means. Shall I scroll through them all or would you like to go straight to the locker?'

'Locker first, please. While I have that dream in my head.'

Everything was how Daphne recalled. The metal box on the top shelf. Two hats and the knife roll directly below. Aprons and two chef's jackets hanging alongside a clothes bag. Three sets of footwear.

'How much can we zoom in?'

'Which part precisely?'

'Bottom row, please.'

There was something odd about the shoes. Not the runners or steeled-capped boots which looked well used and were neatly placed side by side. But the rubber boots were pushed toward the back of the locker and one was on its side, with bits of straw or something sticking out of the sole.

'Is it me or do you think the boots are a couple of sizes larger than the others?'

'Definitely larger.'

'Like mine then. The ones I keep at home to slip in and out of if the garden is wet and I want to wear my thick socks. Susan might put them on if she's going to choose herbs or vegetables because Belle mentioned they grow a lot of their own produce. The mud is most likely from doing that.'

She sighed heavily and leaned back.

'Don't give up, doll. Do you remember how many suspects you had in Little Bridges who turned out to be innocent?'

'At least of murder. A few of them were pretty awful at times. And then my main suspect became a victim of the same killer. But I don't even have a main suspect for Godfrey.'

John pushed the laptop to the middle of the table. 'Would it help to bounce ideas off me? That's if you feel like spending a bit of time on it.'

She almost said no. Rehashing this was exhausting when every clue led to a dead end. If this wasn't Belle's wedding, she'd walk away from the mystery. Go home to Rivers End and spend hours getting their own vegetable garden back into shape.

'Are you up for a drive, love? I have an idea.'

TWENTY-SEVEN

Life with Daphne was never dull. Although he'd always known his high-school sweetheart had a different way of looking at people – and life – than anyone else, it wasn't until they'd begun their travels that John discovered how deeply her intuition and empathy ran beneath the bubbly surface. Let alone her ability to see through lies and find criminals.

Becoming the sidekick of a sleuth hadn't been on his bingo card for life. Any card. He was more comfortable being mister nice guy and was generally logical and calm in nature. Back in Rivers End there'd been a few occasions Daphne had helped friends with their own mysteries but John had managed to stay out of it. For the most part. Over the past months as they faced new situations together, his comfort zone had changed. He'd found himself doing research in the background. Seeing things from Daphne's perspective. And he liked it.

'This is most likely another waste of our time, and I apologise in advance. We should be spending the day sightseeing, since we're leaving tomorrow.'

They were on the road to Crystal Springs for a reason Daphne had yet to explain.

'We are sightseeing, doll.'

'How many times have we gone up and down this road since we arrived? You've not even had a chance to go to photograph the mural in Winton, which was the first thing you planned. I'm being silly so let's go to Winton now.'

They passed Tori's house and both glanced toward it.

'Who could deliberately hit a motorcycle and leave its rider in a ditch?' Daphne's voice almost broke with emotion.

'I wonder if the police have considered a connection between the two?' John had thought about this. 'We don't have many details, but surely two accidents along the same stretch happening to two people with ties to the winery and to each other would raise questions? I know they were three years apart, but still, it seems odd. And you can stop second-guessing yourself, Daphne Jones, and let me in on the plan.'

That made her smile.

John slowed as he caught up a large van with flowers painted all over it.

'Must be the florist. I'll sit behind them.'

'My plan, as you put it, is to work out if it was even possible for Susan to have committed the crime in the time which I've been working on. I thought we could attempt a walk-through of sorts. Retrace the steps it would theoretically have taken to do so in such a short period.'

'Not a bad idea at all.'

'I just feel helpless, love. There's so little information filtering through about how much evidence there really is against Susan or whether there are other people being looked at. We've had almost no interaction with the local police, although those two constables were lovely. Jeremy is a bit scary and he's on my suspect list so I'd rather not speak with him.'

John's experience with the man left a lot to be desired. His so-called statement interview felt eerily like a mild interrogation.

'I wish I hadn't,' he said. 'He was trying to get me to say something negative about Russell and then made it clear he thought Arvin was deceptive. I got the idea he was lining Arvin up as a potential suspect. And so far he hasn't produced a typed statement for me to sign from the recording he made.'

The florist's van turned into the driveway of the winery, stopping at the closed gates. After a moment, they swung open and it went through.

So did John. They were arriving unannounced and uninvited on one of the most important days ever for the family. Keeping a low profile might avoid difficult questions or being drawn away from Daphne's plan.

'Where to?'

'Pinnacle's carpark. I've been looking at Google Earth and know exactly where I want to go.'

Of course you have, you clever cookie.

The van turned off near the lake, slowly crossing the grass.

'Oh, doesn't it look gorgeous!' Daphne craned her neck to see. 'I can't wait to officiate this wedding!'

John only caught a glimpse of colour and movement as he followed the winding road. The carpark had a dozen or so vehicles in it and he deliberately pulled the car into the furthest spot, beneath a tree, hoping it would go unnoticed. He had no idea why, but uneasiness sat in the pit of his stomach. For an instant he reached to turn the motor back on but Daphne was already climbing out.

Seeing how beautiful the wedding area looked almost made Daphne ask John to turn around and head back to Bluebell. Nothing should be allowed to mar this extra special day.

But they *were* here so it was best to get on with things.

'I've got my notebook with everything I've written down since that awful night. I just wondered if first we might take a peek at the vegetable garden and orchard? It might not help, but I have a feeling.'

John had taken his time getting out of the car and locking it but now he nodded. 'And I'm guessing you know where it is?'

'I certainly do, love. Amazing technology available to the average person these days.'

'Not that you're an average person.'

John held his hand out and she took it with a smile. He really was the sweetest man in the whole world.

'We need to head along the path which goes from the restaurant to the cellar door. I think we can take a short cut through the old trees.'

Once they'd walked almost to the cellar door, they deviated to their left and met the path. 'Good. Now, see that side gate through the hedge? We're going to be very cheeky and go through it.'

'The gate which says "No access, private"?'

'I didn't notice a thing.' Daphne pushed open the tall timber gate and they found themselves within sight of a huge orchard behind a fenced area of about half an acre. Inside were garden beds upon garden beds and a huge greenhouse at the very end. 'Now this is what I call a veggie garden!'

The path led all the way to another gate, this time made of steel and wire fine enough to keep rabbits out. Just inside was a shed, presumably to keep gardening tools and the like, along with an impressive panel with a plan of the area for watering.

'I can't imagine the amount of work to keep this so weed-free and thriving but isn't it wonderful?'

'Would you like a tour, Mrs Jones?'

Both of them started as Kenny's head appeared around the corner of the shed. He was grinning.

'Didn't mean to startle you but couldn't help overhearing.'

'Well, that would be nice, thank you.'

Kenny wore overalls and a hat and rubber boots and looked the most relaxed Daphne had ever seen him. He opened the gate and gestured widely. 'This is my second home. Nothing better than fresh from the garden.'

'Totally agree,' John said. 'Back home we grow plenty of produce but nothing on this scale.'

'Or so well set out. Is that scoria instead of grass?'

'Yes. Grass means more mowing but Heather didn't want a concrete jungle either when she designed this. The scoria drains well so even if it's wet we can harvest without getting muddy or slipping, and it's easy enough to weed. Let me show you around.'

Ten minutes later Kenny let them back out of the wire gate. They'd been impressed with the glasshouse and abundance of heirloom varieties of tomatoes and beetroots and range of vegetables.

'You clearly love the garden, Kenny.' Daphne smiled. 'So you help out down here as well as at the restaurant?'

'I like getting soil on my hands. Used to do some work here at the winery on school holidays and enjoyed learning about the care of the vines. Kind of fell into the maître d' role but three or four nights a week is enough working with people.' He laughed shortly. 'Truth be told, plants are less trouble. Eddie and Heather let me make up a full-time job split between the restaurant and here.'

'A bit of a sanctuary?' John asked.

Kenny shuffled his feet, looking down at them. 'Yeah. Something like that. Prefer the plants to some humans.'

Daphne and John exchanged a quick look.

'Well, we've taken up enough of your time, Kenny. I imagine there's still a lot to do before the wedding reception?'

The man raised his head. 'With Susan gone I kinda expected chaos up at Pinnacle but a lot of the work was done when I stuck my head in earlier. Looks like the wedding will go ahead after all.'

'Why wouldn't it, though?'

'No head chef. Guests pulling out. A murder. Isn't that enough?' His expression soured and he turned away. 'Work to do.'

'Thanks for showing us around, Kenny.' Daphne made her tone as bright and friendly as possible.

He grunted in return and disappeared back to the shed.

Daphne slipped her hand through John's arm and directed him away, until out of earshot.

'Did you notice there's no mud here? Nor anything like the straw on the bottom of those other boots.'

'And what was with Kenny's mood change?'

'I think we need to hurry to the top of the stairs for phase two.'

'Phase two' was put on hold when they bumped into Heather coming out of the cellar door. She was struggling under the weight of a wine carton and John immediately took it from her.

'Well you two are the last people I expected this morning!'

Her arms free, she hugged Daphne like a long-lost friend.

'I hope you don't mind us just showing up? We thought... um, we—'

'I'm a bit of an amateur photographer and hoped to take some pictures of the winery... not the wedding parts but the beautiful trees and stone buildings.' John adjusted the box as they reached the ramp.

Thank goodness you have your wits about you!

'Take as many as you want. Are you coming in for some coffee? The kitchen's a bit hectic but I'm sure I can sneak you both a cup.'

'Oh please don't worry. We only had some a little while ago. But I do have a question if you don't mind. Before anyone else is around to hear us.'

Heather gave Daphne an odd look. 'Is it about the locker?'

'We just had a nice chat with Kenny and I noticed he was wearing similar rubber boots to those in Susan's locker.'

'Oh, Susan never wears that kind of boot although most of the vineyard workers and gardeners do. She lives in her work boots or her runners. Nothing else other than the occasional sandals if she's dressing up. But now that you mention it, there *was* a pair in her locker. And the police took them, along with everything else.' She slowed and looked from one to the other. 'This is so confusing.'

'It is very strange. Surely Susan would have noticed them in there if they were planted after the murder but before her arrest.'

They began walking again.

'Only they were pushed to the back of the locker and I had to move all the clothes to one side for John to...'

Whoops. Please don't have been listening to me prattling on.

Heather stopped so abruptly that Daphne almost ran into her. 'I think you have some explaining to do.'

With a small sigh, John put the box onto the stone wall and rubbed his arms. 'Susan called Daphne, almost beside herself because the police were almost there—'

'She called you? Oh my goodness, she must have thought I didn't see her message and was desperate to move the knife roll. Poor Susan.'

'We heard the sirens,' Daphne said. 'I was probably her last resort. She was stressed about her knives mostly, but asked us to remove everything from the locker.'

'But you didn't! If you had she would have been quickly released. And Belle wouldn't be so upset and this wonderful wedding wouldn't be marred by all the scandal!' Heather's face reddened and tears filled her eyes.

Neither Daphne nor John spoke. What was there to say?

'Why did she ask you to take everything? She only asked me to get the knife roll.'

John shrugged. 'What else was in the metal box? Did you know the letters were in there?'

'Not exactly. Susan had mentioned a while ago that she'd received some anonymous and nasty letters but believed ignoring them was the best approach. She said it was probably Godfrey playing one of his silly games. But when I opened her locker it occurred to me those letters might be similar to ours and I took a quick look inside the box. To answer your question, John, she also had other letters, but old handwritten ones from Godfrey, from when they first divorced. And yes, I read them. Every one was an outpouring of his love and deep regret for his part in the end of the marriage. It was only much later, when he finally understood she'd moved on, that he began to do unkind things such as the review.'

Daphne squeezed Heather's hand. 'I'm sorry this has happened to you all.'

Heather squeezed back. 'I shouldn't have snapped at you. For all you both know, Susan might be a killer and you risked being in trouble with the police. Yet you were kind enough to take photos as a record.'

Picking up the box, John continued up the ramp. 'Today is about Arvin and Belle, so we'll drop this off and let you keep getting things ready.'

Daphne agreed. Upsetting Heather wasn't her intention, but now she had another piece of this complicated puzzle.

TWENTY-EIGHT

Managing to avoid seeing anyone else, they made their way to the top of the steps which led to the carpark.

Daphne opened her notebook, flicking through the pages. 'Ah, here we go. I know we're not starting at either the front door or the fire door, but those must only take a moment or two to reach.'

'We can always confirm that later.'

'I have a list of all the people who were either outside or else out of our view from the time of the review to the time we heard him moaning.' Her hand went to her mouth. 'What if he'd just been stabbed and the killer was still there when we called to him?'

John's face was grim. 'And in typical Daphne fashion you barrelled off into the dark and might have run into them.'

'But I didn't. And I can scream like a banshee.'

'This isn't funny.'

'I know, love. And I didn't mean to scare you. In all likelihood the killer was gone or at least far enough away to want to hide, rather than be seen.' She pointed across to the grassy area with the barrier at the edge. 'I'm no forensic expert but there's no obvious damage to that area like someone climbing over might do. Does it make sense to you that Godfrey went down these steps?'

Although John still seemed a bit too serious, he eventually

nodded. 'I've tried to calculate the time between him leaving and the time you found him.'

'You have?'

Finally he grinned and held up his phone. 'Thanks to taking photos and making phone calls that night, I have some data.'

'I love data.'

'Only occurred to me when we were talking to Heather and she mentioned Susan never wearing the rubber boots. Been puzzling over whether those were even meant for her locker and when they were put in it.'

'Wait... you think they belonged to someone else? I suppose a pair might have been left on the floor and someone thought they were hers? This really is just speculation... but what if it was done on purpose? If the boots contain any evidence on the soles, I mean.'

Well this is interesting.

John opened his photos and scrolled, turning the screen so Daphne could see as he went to the images he'd taken of Susan's locker. Most were close-ups but a couple showed the row of a dozen doors. Each with a name at the very top.

'Look at this, Daph. On the right of Susan's is Kenny's locker. What if a pair of his boots ended up in her locker by accident?'

'Oh my. I don't like where my mind is going.'

'That Kenny is the killer? My thought as well. We already know he wears that kind of boot. We know he disappeared right after Godfrey left and was gone for ages. He's an ex-police officer and looks fit. Able to run. And seems to have access to more than just the restaurant.'

A whole shed of sharp gardening tools, for instance.

'What would be his motive?' Daphne looked back in the direction of the fire door. Although not visible from here, it was only around the corner of the building. 'I imagine he could easily have sprinted along this footpath and down the steps. Even collecting that missing knife of Susan's on his way. Let me check when we last saw him.' She turned some pages. 'I've noted seeing him when Godfrey left, because Kenny tried to get payment from him. The first time I noticed he wasn't on the floor was when Jeremy was going, but then he arrived with you and did CPR on Godfrey.'

'Yes, I'd got back to the restaurant to ask for some help finding Godfrey and it was only when I answered your call I noticed he was among the people with me. We were almost at the top of the steps.'

'So he might have appeared from anywhere. Oh dear, Kenny is on my suspect list but I'd almost discarded him. He seems such a nice man.'

And so many killers present as good people. Until you're on their wrong side.

'Shall we time ourselves as if we're Godfrey?' John asked. 'I'll set a stopwatch.'

'Okay, I'll be Godfrey.' Daphne puffed out her chest and deepened her voice. 'All I was doing was joking around and they all got offended.'

With a shake of his head and amusement in his eyes, John held up the phone and started the stopwatch function.

Daphne began the descent at a normal pace because although Godfrey had stormed out of the building, she figured without an audience he'd have slowed enough to take care on what had been slippery steps. Toward the bottom she continued her commentary, patting imaginary coat pockets.

'Where are those keys? Oh that's right, not driving. Jeremy is designated.'

They reached the bottom and Daphne paused.

'What are you doing?'

'Why didn't he go to the car? Did he hear something? Let's pretend he did.' She set off at a faster pace on the narrow path leading to the bushland. 'Hello? Who's there?'

John was right behind her as they passed the sign telling people to turn back.

'Anyone there?'

She stopped where the blood had been pooled on the ground. Now it was barely a stain.

'Stop the watch, love.'

'Just under one minute.'

'Not long at all. And we don't know that he was lured along here. He might have been chased.'

What a dreadful thought.

'The police tape is gone. I guess they've finished any search for the knife or whatever it was.'

'And exactly what do you know about a knife, Mrs Jones?'

Arms crossed, Jeremy stood only a few metres behind them when they spun around in surprise.

'And why are you at the scene of the crime? Again?'

John stepped slightly ahead of Daphne, looking the police officer in the eye and ready to defend his wife. He'd had enough first-hand experience of seeing Jeremy go on the attack and he wouldn't tolerate any bullying behaviour.

'There's no police tape to warn us to keep away,' John said. 'Heather has given me permission to take photographs of the property as part of my hobby.'

'Yet just behind me is a sign explicitly saying not to pass.'

Seeing no point in debating it, John merely offered a friendly smile.

Jeremy's eyes narrowed. 'And the comment about a knife?'

Daphne slipped her arm through John's. 'Has the coroner made any findings yet?'

'I wouldn't tell you if they had. You fancy yourself as some kind of Miss Marple, don't you?'

'Not at all, but I was the person who found poor Godfrey and he spoke to me with his last breaths. I saw both wounds and one was certainly made by a narrow, sharp object. The wound you said didn't exist.'

To Jeremy's credit, he nodded. 'My mistake. I was shocked to see my friend like that and only noticed the bigger wound at the back of his skull.'

'It was a terrible shock,' Daphne said. 'And if John and I hadn't decided to make sure your wife had got to her car safely, we wouldn't have heard Godfrey moaning and he would have died alone.'

'Why would you worry about Aleesha? You didn't know her.'

'She was upset. Had no idea where Godfrey was. And for that matter,' Daphne lifted her chin, 'where were you when she was looking for him?'

Jeremy burst into laughter, throwing his head back and going as far as to pull a handkerchief from a pocket to wipe his eyes. Daphne's hand tightened on John's arm. He knew she wasn't about to back down but she had a soft heart and was easily hurt so the minute this got too much, John was shutting it down.

'Sorry, but that is ridiculous. *You* are questioning *me*?' Jeremy was still grinning.

'It's a simple enough question. You left the restaurant after your wife did. And after Godfrey. Then she returned minutes later looking for Godfrey. Didn't your paths cross? And where was your brother all that time, too, because he was gone before any of you and then was at the scene of the crime before you got there.'

Any amusement – fake or otherwise – vanished, and in place a dark expression sent a shiver down John's spine. Daphne had hit a nerve.

'I'd be careful, Mrs Jones. My family had nothing to do with the murder of our friend. Suggesting otherwise might not end well and—'

'Are you threatening my wife?'

Jeremy's phone started ringing and he impatiently looked at it before glaring at Daphne and John. 'Think what you will. Go back to marrying people, Mrs Jones, and leave the police work to professionals.' He stalked away, stabbing at the phone to answer. 'Yes?'

'I've just put him higher up my suspect list,' Daphne whispered. 'Time to go back to Bluebell.'

· · ·

Jeremy might think he was suitably intimidating but all he'd accomplished was to put himself under Daphne's scrutiny like never before. While John prepared some tea, she had her notebook and scribble pad at hand and was scrolling through his phone in search of photos from the night of the murder. The laptop softly hummed to one side.

'I hadn't realised you took so many.'

'Belle had just stepped back into our lives and I couldn't help snapping away to make sure we went home with more than our memories. Once we're back in Rivers End we can decide which we like best and get some framed.'

'Lovely idea. Oh, thanks. Really need tea right now!' Daphne smiled at John as he found a spot among her things on the table for their cups. 'Sorry about the mess but you can't make an omelette without breaking some eggs.'

'Since when did you use such an old-fashioned saying?'

'Feeling my age, love. Our beautiful foster daughter is getting married today and I'm not as good at solving crime as I once was. Probably time to retire.'

John leaned down to kiss Daphne's lips and then he held her face gently in his hands and gazed at her. 'You've never felt nor acted your biological age and would be bored silly retiring. I think a break over winter at home will have you raring to go again once wedding season comes around next spring. You need a chance to reconnect with your friends and walk on the beach and tend to our beautiful garden.'

She lifted her lips up to kiss him back.

You always know what to say.

'If Belle and Arvin are even half as happy as I am married to you, then they will be blessed on so many levels.'

'And speaking of them, let's find who really killed Godfrey, or at least who framed Susan.' John sat next to her. 'Tell me what to do.'

'Help me go through your photos of that night.'

Daphne made space and in a moment they were clicking on

each photo in turn. Most were just photos of the people at their table, especially once Belle had sat down to eat with them. There were some heartwarming candid shots of Belle and Arvin and a lot of the different courses of food. But some photos picked up what was happening beyond their table.

'This one, John. Perfect shot of Godfrey and his guests. Poor man.' Daphne sighed. 'He had no idea his life was about to taken from him and that he might be sitting near his killer.'

'Sobering thought. Now thanks to the order I took these I'm certain it was after we'd eaten dessert. Yes, see here's a pic of both our sweet treats.'

They clicked through a few more. 'Oh, go back, love. Yes, that one.' Leaning forward to see better, Daphne pointed at the screen. 'No Lainie. My recollection is that she left to have a smoke when the coffee was being brought out. Now that was prior to Arvin showing us all the review, so who else can we see... or not see?'

'Our table had everyone else present. Even though Eddie and Heather aren't visible, they were there. A lot of the tables look empty. Godfrey is staring toward the kitchen, I think.'

Although the focus was a bit blurry, he did seem to be watching in the direction of the kitchen which added weight to the theory he'd made the fake review to stir up Susan.

'Jeremy and Aleesha are talking. Maybe they didn't even know he'd done that. Can you see Warren, love?'

John shook his head then checked the next photo. 'This is the last I took until much later because once Susan came out, every-thing became a bit chaotic. Kenny is in the background, as are the other servers. All clearing tables. Can only see Godfrey from this one so Warren might have been back.'

Daphne screwed up her face in concentration. 'I just don't remember. I'm positive Aleesha left then Godfrey then Jeremy, who paid the bill. Oh, this is getting more confusing by the minute, not easier!'

Her phone rang and with a gasp she answered. 'Susan?'

TWENTY-NINE

'You're on speaker with me and John. Are you alright?' Was it possible Susan had been released?

'I'm at the bench under the willow looking toward the library. Would you mind meeting me here?' Susan's voice was quiet and sounded exhausted.

'On our way, dear.'

The second Daphne disconnected the call she was nudging John along the seat so she could get up.

'I wonder why she didn't just tap on the door? She'd have virtually gone past Bluebell,' John said. He quickly put on shoes while Daphne collected keys and some bottled water from the fridge. 'She didn't sound like herself.'

It only took a couple of minutes to reach the bench in question, which was quite private and offered shade from the late-morning sun. Susan greeted them both with open arms; her eyes were red and puffy.

'Sit down, dear. Have some water. You should have come to the caravan and we'd have made you some tea.'

Taking the water, Susan immediately opened the bottle and drank deeply. She was pale and almost gaunt.

Have you even eaten since being arrested?

Daphne longed to get Susan inside Bluebell and feed her a hearty lunch and copious cups of whichever hot drink she preferred. She pushed the feeling down. There was a reason Susan had asked them to come to her.

'I need to apologise to you both,' Susan said. 'It was wrong for me to ask you to relocate the contents of my locker. Really wrong and you might have been in terrible trouble with the police. I was in utter panic because of certain threats made to me which, admittedly, I hadn't taken seriously. My lawyer used your photographs to show there was no typewriter in my locker at the time of my arrest and I can't tell you how much it means to me that you thought to take them.'

'They really made a difference?' John's eyes brightened. 'I'm so pleased to hear that.'

'The thing is that although they decided not to charge me at this point, Jeremy is determined to find enough evidence. I've been told not to approach you two which is why I thought this would be better. Just an accidental meeting, if anyone saw us.' Susan suddenly looked around and then over to the carpark near the library. Nobody was around. 'And I can't go to work. Not even for the wedding.'

Tears welled in her eyes and she grasped one of Daphne's hands.

'This is so unfair. I'd never hurt Godfrey.'

'And we believe you, dear. In fact, we've been trying to work out who did have the opportunity and motive to do that dreadful thing and it would be so helpful if I could ask a couple of questions? If you feel up to it?'

Susan laughed without any humour and released Daphne's hand. 'There's nothing you could ask which the police haven't and probably more than once, so please, what are your questions?'

I hadn't expected this opportunity and have to tread lightly.

Daphne's mind darted back to her early notes and then the more recent clues which had muddied the metaphorical waters.

Deciding to start with the obvious, she offered what she hoped was an encouraging smile.

'After you and Godfrey had words, you hurried back to the kitchen. I mean, I can only imagine how distressing his review was.'

'I'm used to it. He is... was always trying to get my attention instead of simply accepting our marriage was really over. He didn't have a violent bone in his body but he could be quite verbally cutting when things didn't go his way. But yes, I was mad because I'd let him get under my skin and I'd made a scene in the restaurant I love so much. So I went down to the vegetable garden to cool off. There was no more food to cook and the best thing for me was a quick walk.'

'Understandable. How did you find out about the review?' John asked.

Good question, love!

'Lainie.'

'Lainie? How did she know? Did she just walk in and tell you?'

'No, she'd never speak directly to me if she could avoid it. Can't stand how rude she is to people she believes are beneath her or stop her plans. I saw her in the doorway showing something on her phone to Marie, who is one of the line cooks, and went to tell her to leave but she disappeared pretty fast. It was Marie who told me about the review, and she was really upset about it which is partly why I reacted so badly.' Susan looked down at her hands. 'My team mean everything to me. I should have stayed in the kitchen, then I wouldn't have been arrested and be needing to defend myself instead being there for Belle.'

'There are still a few hours until the wedding, dear. Never say never.'

After glancing at her watch, Susan stood. 'I wish. But Belle doesn't need any further drama and I'm in desperate need of a shower and sleep.'

Daphne and John got to their feet.

'Please keep in touch, dear, and if there's anything we can do, just phone.'

'You've done so much. But you can give Belle an extra hug from me.'

'Oh, I'll definitely do that. Just before you leave... there were a lot of people in and out of the restaurant before and after Godfrey left. I know you went to the vegetable garden but I was wondering whether you happened to notice anyone else?'

Susan thought for a moment then gave a small nod. 'Someone was leaving the barrel room through the side door. It was raining by then and hard to see but I assumed it was Claude because he sometimes stays late when he's working on a vintage. Then I heard noises from the steps and around the carpark, people talking loudly and urgently but from where I was it was impossible to see or hear what was happening so I started to run back. There was nobody in the kitchen nor the restaurant so I went back outside to phone Heather.'

'But she didn't answer.'

'No. I think like everyone else she was too focused on Godfrey but I didn't know about it until Belle came to tell me.'

'There was nobody lurking around the kitchen or the building later who shouldn't be there?'

'It is such a blur, Daphne. The only odd thing was...' She creased her forehead. 'Several of the lockers – including mine – were slightly open when I came in the next morning. Actually no, Friday morning. I don't even know why I use the padlock as everyone knows the combination. I closed them all and put my dry-cleaned dress for the wedding into mine. I'd actually forgotten about this until just now. I really do need to go home before I fall asleep on my feet.'

After another round of hugs, Susan shuffled away.

Daphne wandered to the edge of the water and gazed in.

'What are you thinking, doll?'

That I've never dealt with such a confusing and puzzling crime.

'Why would those lockers be open?'

'Someone looking for something?'

'Or putting a pair of muddy boots into one of them. Looking

for the right locker and maybe not noticing the names at the top. Perhaps interrupted and tossed them into Susan's. I think if we can find that person, we might find the killer, love.' Daphne pointed to reeds growing along the bank. 'And possibly even the murder weapon.'

THIRTY

The boathouse and lake looked like a fairy tale. Rows of seats were decorated with emerald green or burgundy bows. A dozen potted white roses in full bloom lined either side of the seats, with long pots filled with brightly coloured hyacinths in between each rose. The boatshed was equally pretty draped in long garlands of flowers, and the podium almost took Daphne's breath away.

Nobody else was around, which was ideal for her purpose of coming so early, but first she had to take a closer look at the spot where she'd marry Belle and Arvin in just a couple of hours.

'Isn't this divine, love?'

John followed her to the low, round raised podium. Built around and over it was a three-way arch, covered in more roses and an ornamental grapevine.

'Perfect for the setting, Daph. Roses are so important at wineries as they show disease faster than grapevines, thus helping the grape growers keep the plants healthy. And the sun will be sinking, which should make everything look a bit magical.'

'All for our Belle.' Daphne kept a tight grip on emotions which were already threatening to turn into tears. 'The most important wedding I've ever officiated...'

'I want to hug you but worry I'll crease your lovely suit.'

'Hug away. This material is pretty resilient.'

She'd chosen soft linen pants in dark grey and an even darker jacket, over a white silk blouse. They'd come from one of the newer boutiques in Rivers End, run by two local fashion designers who genuinely cared about natural fabrics and timeless styles.

As if to prove her point, Daphne cuddled against John's chest, her arms around his waist. 'I love you, John Jones.'

His warm eyes filled her heart with joy. 'And I love you, too. More today than on our own wedding day, if that's even possible.'

'It is. Having you by my side on this journey through life is more than I could ever have dreamed up. And I adore being on the road with you and Bluebell, even if I'm a bit homesick at the moment.'

He kissed her forehead. 'We'll fix that quickly.'

'But first we have to catch a killer.'

'Which you say in the same matter-of-fact way as you'd announce dinner is served.'

'Oh, I feel quite overstimulated about the rest of the day, so best I keep a calm exterior.' For a moment she closed her eyes and leaned against John, safe in his arms. This was her harbour. But time was against them and she had to focus on the job at hand.

A moment later they were walking around the lake, as close to the banks as was practical.

Do not get these shoes wet or muddy, Daph!

'Stay away from the edge, John. You look so nice in that suit and I'd hate for your pants to get wet.'

'Yes, dear.' John winked at her.

They reached the furthest end of the lake from the boathouse and stopped, watching ducks paddling in and out of the reeds.

'Do you have your phone?'

'Never far away. I gather you'd like another look at those rubber boots in Susan's locker?'

'Great minds do think alike.'

Ever since she'd seen the close-up of the rubber boots, particu-larly the one on its side, Daphne had puzzled over what was sticking to the mud on the sole. The vegetable garden was a false start.

'A red herring.'

'What is?'

'I said that aloud, didn't I? I was thinking that checking the vegetable garden to match the debris on the boot didn't solve anything.'

'Lots of red herrings recently. Might as well write a book or make a mystery movie with all the twists and turns.' John turned the phone. 'Zoomed-in image focusing on the sole.'

Stepping carefully, Daphne went as close to the water as she dared and managed to grab the top of a reed and snap it off. John grabbed her hand to help her back up as her shoes began sinking. 'Whoops. I might need to give these a clean before the ceremony.' She lifted a foot, turning it to see the underside. 'Actually, would you take a photo please?'

'Of your foot?'

'The sole of the shoe. Here, I'll balance better... be quick!'

Almost hopping on her left foot as she held up her right, Daphne nearly toppled over but sheer determination to get the photo kept her upright.

'Done.'

'Whew. Not as athletic as I used to be.'

John sniggered.

'If you weren't holding your phone I would poke you with this reed. We both know I've always been built for comfort, not speed, but let me have my moment of fantasy.'

'In that case I'll make sure to keep the phone on me at all times. But seriously, look at this.'

The photograph showed a bit of mud and small, straw-like pieces of reed attached.

'There's bits all through the softer ground.' She held up the thin reed. 'I guess parts break off.'

John went back to the boots. 'I reckon you've found the source. Would love to put these side by side on a bigger screen to compare.

The question is, why was someone down here wearing those rubber boots?'

'To dispose of the murder weapon. Not the most original place but if it was a crime of opportunity, then the killer might not have had many options or much time.'

'And another question... who was wearing them?'

'Either the killer or their accomplice.' Daphne stared at the lake. Somewhere in its depths was likely a murder weapon and if she wasn't mistaken, it was one of Susan's knives. How horribly ironic that a gift Godfrey had given his wife was the tool which killed him. 'I'm almost certain two people are involved.'

'Shall we go back to the car while you explain?'

'In a minute, if you don't mind. I'd like to walk from here to the place Godfrey died first. See how easy it would be to get here from there.'

'I'm listening, Daph.'

She drew a quick breath. 'It has always felt that this murder was part opportunity and part planned. Who knew he was likely to post such a scathing review? Godfrey's review might have fallen flat. Susan might not have seen it or even if she had, perhaps she'd ignore it. There is a degree of engineering the situation in the background, so I'm not convinced Godfrey was the target, as such.'

'So he wasn't killed because of a grudge or with specific intention. More that he was in the right place at the right time for the killer?'

'Exactly. If that is the case, only so much could be planned. If Susan appearing to argue with him was the hope, then it wouldn't give the killer much time to somehow get into the kitchen and steal a knife from a knife roll. I don't know if you noticed but there were several people from the kitchen who were watching from the hallway when she came out.'

'I did. Which might well have left the kitchen empty... but only for a minute. If that.'

'Then we could rule out anyone who was physically present in the restaurant at the time of the confrontation.'

John tilted his head. 'Unless they already had the knife.'

'A line cook? Dishwasher?'

'Hmm. I'd imagine the police spoke to them all and certainly Susan seems to live for her staff. Heather as well.'

'Yes, and Belle adores each and every one of them. Let's pop them on the "come back if all else fails" shelf for now.' Daphne smiled. 'I think someone got hold of the knife, knowing full well which one was best for the intended job, and was able to use that minute or so when the kitchen was empty. Stealing it earlier ran the risk of Susan noticing it was gone.'

'Do you think they passed it to the killer?'

'That is an excellent question. And one I can't answer yet. Do you mind using your stopwatch again? Not that I can walk as fast as someone who might be fleeing a crime scene. Not in these shoes.' She glanced down and frowned. 'I will have to give them a clean.'

The strangest sensation prickled at Daphne's neck and upper back. A feeling of being watched. Slowly she raised her head and gazed around but the only person in sight was her husband. This was all getting to her and the sooner they got some answers, the better.

All the walking this week was helping his waistline. Up and down steps, ramps, across wide stretches of undulating grass, various paths, and in and out of town from the little island where Bluebell was parked. John patted his stomach, pleased he'd fitted so well back into this suit after months of it being just a fraction too tight.

'Are you feeling unwell, love?'

'Not in the least. I should have left my jacket in the car.'

'Should we go there first?'

'I might just carry it for now.' He handed Daphne his phone, with the stopwatch counting, and shrugged out of the jacket as they walked. 'I'm not sure if we need to time this. Not like we're running from the scene of a crime.'

'True.' She handed back the phone. 'It isn't an exact science.'

They'd left the lake across the grass and were almost where the wide driveway split in three directions.

'This is the most direct route, otherwise you'd need to go through gates and wind around the vines on both sides.' Daphne pointed ahead. 'If we can see the restaurant then presumably we're visible to anyone looking this way. And that makes me wonder why risk coming down a highly visible road to dispose of a murder weapon in the lake?'

'There's lots of solar lighting along here and it didn't start raining until after you found Godfrey, so not a lot of cover,' John said. 'Plus there was the chance of cars heading out from the carpark. And the need to pass the gate leading to Eddie and Heather's private grounds and house to our left.'

Still walking at a quick pace, they entered the road to the restaurant carpark and then turned onto the bush track.

'No need to go further, John. Let's go and put your jacket in the car.'

Daphne stopped in the middle of the road.

'What are you thinking, doll?'

'I'm trying to imagine I'm fleeing the scene of a crime and have to remain unseen at all costs. Now, I could try and scramble up the hill through all that heavy scrub but risk getting filthy and wet and even scratched to pieces, which would be a giveaway.' She gestured down the slope. 'As much as I believe the knife is in the lake, running down there when people are out looking for Godfrey is asking to be caught.'

On the move again, Daphne led the way back to the main driveway and gestured to the left.

'We've never driven to the cellar door parking area but we know it's directly along here. And although it passes the restaurant carpark, there's this thick hedge all the way along.'

Ah... I see where you're going with this.

'It would be almost a direct route from where Godfrey died to the cellar door. Is the knife hidden in there?'

The glint in Daphne's eyes told John she was finally putting the pieces together.

'The knife is in the lake. But I think it was hidden in a hurry elsewhere then moved when the person thought it safe to do so. And not the cellar door.'

They walked through the carpark so John could leave his jacket.

'Then where? Not the vegetable garden because Susan would have crossed paths with them and she... oh.'

'Oh, indeed.' Daphne was grinning ear to ear.

'She saw someone come out of the barrel room.'

'And I remembered something else. When Claude and Arvin had that heated argument the other day, I distinctly heard Arvin say he had not left the side door unlocked. That was on Thursday, presumably about the previous day. The boots appeared in Susan's locker on Friday, to the best of our knowledge.'

John hung his jacket in the car. 'Do you want to leave yours as well?'

'No, all good.' Her forehead was deeply creased in concentration. 'Someone had access to the kitchen to get the knife. The barrel hall to hide the knife. And the staff room to stash the boots. I'm dreadfully afraid this is pointing back to Kenny. Except I still can't work out why. Is this all tied up with those letters or something completely different?'

'Has to be the letters, seeing as the typewriter was planted in Susan's locker,' John said.

'Tying a murder to Crystal Springs and long-running threats to Susan, the head chef. Great way to stop guests coming, let alone what would happen to their wine lovers' retreat.'

'Shall we head up to the restaurant and get some refreshments? Heather said to drop in any time this afternoon.' Getting Daphne to sit for a bit and think was the best thing right now. He could see the frustration in her face. 'You're doing great.'

Although she nodded, and accepted the hand he offered, she didn't look convinced.

THIRTY-ONE

Halfway up the steps, Daphne stopped, gazing toward the restaurant. There was laughter and music drifting out; a reminder of the importance of today for the special family who owned and loved this property. They and Belle deserved answers. So did Susan, who'd been such a big part of the wedding planning and was missing both the ceremony and the joy of cooking the reception meals. None of this was fair. A person or persons were doing a good job of destroying the hard work of generations of the Kingsleys.

There was still time to give the police names or evidence or a well-considered theory which might be enough for them to soften their stance on Susan. Even if just for today.

'Did we forget something?'

'I might put my jacket in the car after all. And collect my notebook. I left it inside my bigger bag.'

'Okay, I'll run down and—'

'No, no. Let me. A moment to myself might help my mood, love. I'll catch right up.'

John handed her the car keys with an understanding smile. 'See you very soon.'

There were a dozen or so vehicles in the carpark now and

theirs was the furthest, under the tree John favoured. Daphne wasn't in a hurry. Her thoughts were bouncing all over the place. Having her notebook might help her compose herself, because sooner or later she'd need to change her mindset and be a celebrant, rather than a sleuth.

'Mrs Jones?'

Hand outstretched to unlock the car, Daphne almost dropped the keys as Warren Karlson appeared from behind a van she'd just passed.

'Could we have a chat?'

He looked friendly enough. The same smile she'd seen almost every time they'd met, other than the first night.

'I'm just leaving my jacket in the car then meeting my husband up at Pinnacle. You're welcome to come with me and we can all talk.'

'Not much time, I'm afraid. It really is just something I want to address. Something Jeremy mentioned to me and I've found quite upsetting.' The smile vanished and he took a step closer. 'You've cast aspersions on me.'

'I have?'

'Jeremy said you suspect me in Godfrey's death. Me. One of his friends.'

Although her heart was pounding, Daphne was fascinated by the man's approach. If he was innocent, wouldn't he just ignore what people said? Or, at worst, get a lawyer to send a letter? She knew she was safe. It was broad daylight and there were people around, including John, who'd come looking soon if she didn't appear.

'Were you watching us near the lake earlier?'

His eyes narrowed.

'Because I was certain someone was around. Were you worried we might find it?'

A deep red flush rose up his neck and right to his forehead, but he didn't move or answer.

'Jeremy assured me that none of his family could possibly be involved in murder. Does that mean he doesn't know, or that he's a consummate liar?'

'You don't understand what's been going on for years. These people are making it impossible for anyone else to make a buck.'

'These people? The Kingsley family?'

He nodded.

'They seem so nice.'

'Sure. To your face. But then Eddie uses his contacts on the council to get what he wants and at the same time shuts down other people's dreams.' Any pretence of being civil was gone. Warren's face was twisted in anger. 'His precious retreat is all that matters and even Godfrey helped him by supporting his application and then turning other councillors against ours. Godfrey, who was my friend and not even married to Susan anymore.'

That's right. Godfrey was a council member. So this was more than an opportunistic murder. You had a grudge.

'I can't imagine how upsetting that must have been. Can't you take it to VCat though? I know a few developers who got council approval after appealing to a higher government power.'

'No idea what VCat is. And don't bother explaining because it doesn't matter anymore. After today I foresee Crystal Springs going on the market at a bargain price and we're poised to pick it up for a song.'

Who is 'we'?

A chill went up Daphne's spine.

'Today is Belle and Arvin's wedding day.'

'Not if nobody can marry them.'

'I'm going to go now.' Daphne took a big step back. 'I won't cause you any trouble.'

'Nah, we don't believe that. Snooping around, asking questions, even meeting up with Susan when she's meant to keep away. Yeah, I've been watching you because Lainie warned me you were trouble. But not for much longer.'

A burst of laughter up at Pinnacle took Warren's attention for a second and that was all Daphne needed. She knew she couldn't get past him to the steps and the van behind him had its side door wide open. A sharp dart of fear forced her legs into action and she was running in the opposite direction as fast as she could.

'Get back here!'

'Haaalp! Haaalp!'

Almost immediately she was out of the carpark and racing across soft grass. This was where she'd followed Belle the very first day and she knew where she was heading. But the man behind her was faster and younger and stronger.

What have I done? Oh, John, what have I done?

THIRTY-TWO

Heart thudding a million miles an hour, Daphne threw herself against the trunk of the massive old oak. From behind her came a sliding sound and a slam. Warren had gone to close the door of the van. But no motor had started so he wasn't driving around looking for her.

She got her bearings. To her left, somewhere through more trees and up a hill which quickly steepened, was the ramp up to the restaurant. But first was a long path and lots of places to be caught in the open. Directly ahead though was the cellar door – which was closed – and beside that, the barrel hall.

As the heaving of her chest lessened, Daphne felt for her phone. The car keys were gone, probably dropped near the car. But her phone was safe in her pocket and as she drew it out, a twig snapped nearby. Holding a hand over her mouth to stop a cry coming out, she started running again, sprinting between and around trees then across the second carpark.

She raced through the huge open doors of the heart of the winery... the massive barrel hall where oak casks stretched as far as the eye could see. She aimed for the furthest end where stainless steel vats towered above her. Perfect to hide behind.

A small hope that Claude would be here evaporated. She was alone.

Her shoes were loud and she stopped and slipped them off. The ground was cold but easy enough to walk on and at least she was quiet now. Or would be once she caught her breath.

Finally reaching the massive vats, Daphne found a narrow walkway running between them and the thick stone wall. The gloom made it a slow shuffle until she figured she was about halfway along.

Surely from here she wouldn't be seen if she sent a text message? The options were disappearing fast. This time she got the phone out and made sure it was on silent mode before typing a message to John and sending it. And then two more to the other people who might see it if he didn't. In the moment or two which lit up around her, she realised there was a door just a bit further along.

If I can open it, then I can sneak out.

'Mrs Jones.'

Daphne jumped and almost dropped her phone.

His voice echoed. How close was he?

'There's no way out.'

Oh, yes there is. Not only do I know there's a side door somewhere but now I've found a back exit.

She edged closer to the door.

'We might as well have a face-to-face conversation. Make an agreement.'

With a killer? Not likely.

His voice was closer and a flashlight lit the end of the narrow walkway. Daphne was at the door, her fingers reaching for the handle.

'It doesn't have to be this way. Daphne. May I call you that?'

As if she'd answer such a question. She pushed the handle down. It barely moved. Then up. The same. If it was locked then what could she do? Her legs were shaking from all the running and probably the adrenaline. If she had to run more he'd catch her. And if she tried climbing the ladder up the side of the steel vat? Like in her dream?

It didn't bear considering. With stockinged feet she'd have no chance on these thin rungs and climbing when she had hardly any breath was a ridiculous notion.

'What if I offer you money? A lot of money. Lainie is filthy rich, thanks to an inheritance and although she wants to be richer, she'd happily spend some of it not to be in jail. For your silence on the matter we can give you ten thousand dollars. That's a lot for a pensioner.'

Pensioner!

Clearly Lainie was the brains behind this and Warren was the brawn. If she was right, she'd string him along for a bit. Give people a chance to rescue her before she ended up in a vat of red wine.

'Alright. Don't come any closer and I'll negotiate.'

Her hands returned to the door handle and she began slowly moving it up and down, hoping it wouldn't squeak.

'What about fifteen thousand?'

'No, I don't want money, dear. There's two things I do want though, and if you've done any research on me then you know I keep my promises.'

She wanted to cross her fingers but needed them for the door.

Warren laughed. 'No money? Go on.'

'First thing and this is very important. I want Belle and Arvin's wedding to go ahead today as planned and for no harm to ever come to either of them.'

There was a sigh. 'Sure. Let the kids have their moment.'

The handle was moving a bit more freely. It wasn't locked but rusty.

'Thank you, Warren. The second thing is purely for my own curiosity. You've already worked out I am a bit of an amateur sleuth. A bit of a Miss Marple.' She screwed up her face because although she loved Miss Marple and everything Agatha Christie, all she was doing was recycling Jeremy's words. 'I'm just interested in how you did it. Normally I can work out a mystery quite quickly but you and Lainie have completely stumped me!'

Best actor award goes to Daphne Jones.

She quickly tapped video on her phone, put it on the floor, and returned to working on the handle.

'That's all you want? And you'll leave after the wedding and never say a word?'

'It would make an... old woman happy.'

'I should check with Lainie first.'

'Really? It is obvious you are the brains here. The smart one. Look how well you've fooled everyone.'

The long pause was a worry. Had she overdone the false compliments?

'Yeah. Okay, sure. Lainie and me are a couple. Russell doesn't know. Not yet. I've worked for ten years building my business and people like Eddie and Heather just use us. Anyway, Lainie bought a winery on the other side of town years ago. She isn't interested in wineries but the land has natural springs and she knows the beauty industry. When we heard on the grapevine what was in the planning for here, she immediately realised how much money we could make by getting in first and taking the town by storm. Told you, she's already rich but wants to be one of them billionaire types with a yacht one day. When she applied to the council to build a retreat and spa they'd just approved Eddie's, and Godfrey made sure there wasn't competition by opposing Lainie.'

At last the handle was really moving. Just not enough to open the door.

'Lainie approached Eddie and Heather to buy Crystal Springs after he had his accident and was told no. She doesn't take no for an answer though. Her winery needed an edge, and Russell suggested Claude, but he won't leave. So we figured we'd make Crystal Springs a monumental failure and started sending letters to people. To Eddie. To the owner of a local beauty salon who was set to head up the one here. To Susan.'

'Why Susan?'

Another silence except there was a footfall here and there. He was moving closer.

'Got Russell to work on Claude again a couple of months back. He still wasn't budging. It was like the Kingsleys were too stupid to work out that they needed to pack it in. Either give up the retreat or the winery. Or both. So we tried another tactic. Figured Susan was an insider. Might do some damage for us. Instead she ignored the letters. They all did, and that meant we had to show them consequences.'

'The road accidents. But what about Godfrey? How on earth did you make it happen? I'm in awe of such clever planning.'

'That was my idea. I stirred Godfrey up. Made the booking. Told him it was time to make Susan realise how much she'd hurt him. Lainie just waited until the review was live then went to the kitchen and made sure Susan found out. Then the minute all hell broke loose and the kitchen was empty, Lainie strolled back in and selected one of Susan's knives.' Warren's voice was proud. 'I was outside and she handed it me and I hid at the bottom of the steps until he came out. Knew he had a temper and would storm out of Pinnacle alone. Minute he saw me I held up the knife and he ran. You know what happened next.'

'My goodness. That was A-class planning. But then you had knife to get rid of.'

'And a rock. He staggered away after I used the knife and was on his knees making too much noise. One hard whack with a rock and he was out but then I had two things to get rid of. Damned rain and people driving home changed my plans. I hid it in here. I have a key to lots of the property, thanks to Kenny.'

'Kenny?'

Warren's laugh was sickening. 'Jeremy caught him red-handed stealing from a crime scene once and has held it over Kenny's head for years. Amuses Jeremy to bully him, but made my life easier because I told Kenny he could help me or I'd have a quiet word with my brother.'

Oh, that poor man. He's been used for too long.

'Then you collected the knife and rock and tossed them into the lake.'

'That was Lainie. She got impatient waiting for me to move them at my leisure and took my keys and came here before dawn on Friday. Found some boots then had the clever idea of putting them in Susan's locker. Almost got caught when someone arrived early. But worth it because it helped get Susan arrested.'

The handle had loosened yet still wouldn't open. Daphne was certain it wasn't locked and began applying more pressure.

'Well, putting the typewriter in the locker was a stroke of genius. Blame Susan for all the letters typed on it.'

'My idea.'

'Obviously.'

Silence fell... other than the faint sound of footsteps. Daphne jiggled the handle more vigorously.

'See, I don't believe you'll keep quiet, Mrs Jones.'

She jumped almost out of her skin. He was on the ledge only a few metres away.

'I made a promise, dear.'

'People don't keep promises. Now, we're going to quietly walk back to my van. Or I can knock you out right here and carry you.'

Daphne scooped up her phone and shoved it in her pocket.

Warren's eyes glinted above his flashlight.

You are not going to kill me!

She put all of her strength into forcing the handle up again, and then down, and this time something gave.

'No, you don't.'

He lunged forward and she threw her shoulder against the door. It opened with a loud groan and she fell into the sunlight, onto grass.

As she scrambled to her feet, Warren grabbed her and she screamed with all her might.

He tried to cover her mouth and she kicked his shin.

'Get your hands off me! Haaalp!'

In a blur of movement there were suddenly other people there.

Arvin, Owen, Brent, Claude, all pulling Warren away from her. And then John. A siren wailed in the distance.

'She said to get your hands off her.'

His arm swung backwards and then as if in slow motion, John's fist came forward and smashed into Warren's nose. The man crumpled to the ground and John looked at his hand in shock.

'John?'

Daphne threw her arms around him and then he was holding her so tightly she could barely breathe. And that's when the tears began.

THIRTY-THREE

John only let Daphne out of his sight long enough for her to freshen up in the ladies' room, and that was after Heather promised to go with her. They'd had some frights over the years but today was one he'd never forget. He gingerly extended his fingers, thankful of the bandage applied by the paramedic who'd checked him earlier.

He was at a table outside Pinnacle, cups of steaming coffee waiting for Daphne's return. In the distance, the sun was making a slow descent to the horizon, which meant the wedding was less than an hour away. As pretty as the outlook was, he wished he was driving home with his girl. Go back to Rivers End and never leave.

'Can't wrap her up, John.' Eddie wheeled to the table. 'Here's some mini eclairs to give you both a sugar hit. Get you through the next couple of hours until Susan can feed you.'

'Wait... Susan?'

'Constable Woodcroft was on the phone while Warren was being taken away and she then told me her boss had rescinded all conditions of Susan's release.'

Best news all day. Although finding a killer comes close.

Eddie gestured to the restaurant. 'Tonight we're going to celebrate more than a much-wanted wedding. Thanks to you and

Daphne, we're free of the threats and pressures applied by those two... Well, I can't call them what I'm thinking, but you get the drift. And I've never met anyone so brave as your wife.'

John couldn't speak. She was brave. She'd fought back in the only way she knew... challenging a killer.

'I'd never want to be on her wrong side. Videoing almost the entire confession he gave her? Texting you and Arvin and Constable Woodcroft with her location was smart. And despite the terrible danger he put her in, she wasn't going to go quietly.'

Finally, John chuckled. Quiet was not a word he'd have used. 'Heard her first call for help and we were already on our way but we went to the restaurant's carpark.'

His heart had plummeted finding the car keys on the ground. But then her text came and Arvin led them all to the disused door at the back of the building.

'Don't know what to do about Kenny.' Eddie's shoulders dropped. 'He might not have personally done anything wrong, other than give Warren a set of keys, but he kept secrets which might have stopped Tori's accident and Godfrey's death. Difficult to imagine keeping him on.'

'And Jeremy? Still says he had nothing to do with anything?'

'We'll see. He'll have some explaining to do around his handling of our letters, and the whole investigation of Godfrey's murder. Not at all convinced he didn't suspect Warren was up to no good.' Eddie rolled his eyes. 'And as for my wife! Hiding Susan's precious knives and stuff inside a waterproof bag in one of the vats.'

They both laughed and the weight slowly lifted from John's shoulders.

'Claude had a word with me. After the arrest. Said Russell's been pressuring him to go work for Lainie. Russell even told him we wanted him gone to give Alvin the reins. All lies, but it explains Claude being out of sorts so much lately. As for Lainie, we never knew it was her who'd bought the old winery but it kind of makes sense now. Knowing there was greed involved. And a grudge.'

'So is Claude leaving?'

'Nope. He's committed to staying another five years and I'm thinking of offering him a share of the winery.'

John held out his fingers again.

'Satisfying?' Eddie grinned.

'I've never hit anyone in my life. Probably never will again because it hurts like the devil.'

But immensely satisfying. Not that I'll say it aloud.

'Will you reconsider leaving Benalla tomorrow? Heather and I... well, we feel like you and Daphne are old friends and we'd enjoy having some time to show you more of our home and town.'

'We feel the same way about you both. But Rivers End is calling and we need a bit of time to let the dust settle.'

'But we'll come back soon!' Daphne was smiling as she sat at the table.

Her colour was normal again and she'd stopped trembling but there was still wariness in her eyes. John gently pushed her coffee closer to her.

'Thanks, love. But now Belle is firmly part of our lives again we will make regular trips up. And if you and Heather can get away sometime, we'd love to show you our little town.'

Arvin's head appeared through the open door. 'Dad? We all need help with our ties. And we need to hurry up and get down to the lake. We can't be late!'

Eddie smiled as he turned the wheelchair. 'On my way, lad.' He looked over his shoulder. 'See you down there. And remember what I said, John.'

Once they were alone, Daphne carefully took John's injured hand. 'You really are my hero. What did Eddie say?'

'Lots. All complimentary. They feel like a weight has lifted.'

She nodded. 'No more threatening letters. No more murders and people working against the family. I wonder how Russell will cope though. Not only finding out his girlfriend was also with someone else, but that she was actively hurting people his daughter cared about. I feel sorry for Marsha as well.'

'Oh, don't. Apparently she was helping her mother and it was her idea to take Tori's place. They were convinced ruining this wedding would be the last nail in the coffin for the family and if the wedding wasn't stopped by Warren taking you out of the picture, she was going to steal Tilly. Everyone knows how much Belle and Heather love that horse so it would have been impossible for the wedding to happen until she was located.'

'How dare they! What kind of monster would steal a perfectly innocent animal just to hurt someone? Can you please show me how to punch, because I want to find Lainie and Marsha and give them something to remember me by!'

It was all John could do not to burst into laughter but Daphne's righteous anger was too real to ignore.

He got to his feet and held out his arms. 'We should get you down to the boathouse. And no, I won't show you how to punch people. But yes, it would have been a heinous crime.'

'You think I'm ridiculous.'

Daphne pushed back her chair and stood.

'Not even close. I think you are courageous and kind and generous and loving.'

'Well, that's better.' She stepped into his embrace.

Holding her against his chest, John wanted to protect her from the world. Keep her to himself and never allow her near another wedding unless it was one of their friends in Rivers End. But Daphne was her own person and had her own choices to make.

'I'll never put myself in so much danger again. I'm so sorry you were so scared for my safety.'

That would do for now. He let out a long sigh.

An alarm on her phone went off. 'Time to go, love.'

With late afternoon sunlight streaming through the trees as a backdrop, Tilly looked like a dream-horse as she walked across the soft grass with ribbons in her mane and tail and a beautiful bride on her back.

Susan and Heather were there to meet her and Claude came to

take Tilly while Belle's dress was smoothed and a bouquet provided. Then Susan and Heather accompanied Belle to where a long carpet formed an aisle.

Russell walked toward her and then deviated to one of the rows. He leaned down to speak to someone... it was hard to see from where Daphne waited at the podium. The person stood and followed Russell to meet Belle. One on each side of her, they waited for the music to begin.

Tears poured down Daphne's face. It was John on one side and his smile was so wide that the horrible events earlier in the day vanished.

The music started, the guests stood, and the wedding began.

Arvin also had tears as his bride approached and with a grin, Rhianna forced a tissue into his hand and then gave a couple to Daphne. She quickly dried her face and as Belle stopped in front of her groom, the love in the air was tangible. This was her foster child. Happy and embarking on a new life.

I am the luckiest woman alive.

John smiled at her before he and Russell returned to their chairs.

No, I am the luckiest person alive.

EPILOGUE

The first view of Rivers End always took Daphne's breath away and today was no different. John must have felt the same way, pulling into the carpark above the beach where they both climbed out.

Hand in hand they walked to the edge of the cliff and drank in the beauty of this place they'd called home for most of their lives.

The breeze picked up, a little colder than expected.

'Not long until the seasons change,' Daphne said. 'Have to get started on setting up the veggie garden for winter.'

'I foresee hearty meals and reading in the evening beside a crackling fireplace.'

'And long walks on the beach.'

'Catching up with our friends.'

'This is where my heart is, John.' Daphne rested her head on his shoulder. 'Rivers End with you by my side.'

'I feel the same.' His arm slipped around her waist.

Down on the beach, a lone surfer twisted and turned on a wave as a woman watched from the sand, sitting with an arm around a golden retriever.

We will travel again. But for now I can't imagine anywhere I'd rather be.

'Shall we take Bluebell home?'
'Just a few minutes more, love. Just a few minutes more.'

A LETTER FROM THE AUTHOR

My heartfelt thanks for reading *Of Vines and Victims*. I hope you loved joining Daphne on this new adventure. If you want to join other readers in hearing all about my new releases and bonus content, you can sign up for my newsletter.

www.stormpublishing.co/phillipa-nefri-clark

If you enjoyed this book and could spare a few moments to leave a review, that would be hugely appreciated. Even a short review can make all the difference in encouraging a reader to discover my books for the first time. Thank you so much.

It was an absolute delight to return to the travelling life of Daphne, John and Bluebell in this brand-new story. I'd had it in mind for a long time to write about finding Belle. Daphne's own upbringing wasn't the best and fostering gave her and John the opportunity to shower love and care on children in times of need. The connection with Belle was special and now that they've reunited, I feel Daphne finally has a missing part of herself returned and she is stronger for it. I hope you have enjoyed this latest adventure and thank you for coming along on this special journey.

Thanks again for being part of this amazing journey with me and I hope you'll stay in touch – I have so many more stories and ideas to entertain you with! From my heart to yours.

Phillipa

KEEP IN TOUCH WITH THE AUTHOR

www.phillipaclark.com

instagram.com/phillipanefriclark

facebook.com/PhillipaNefriClark

ACKNOWLEDGMENTS

First and foremost I have to thank my wonderful and incredibly patient editor, Emily Gowers, for allowing me some extra time to write Daphne's new book. I'd hit a bit of a roadblock thanks to some curve-balls from life, but Emily reminded me to take Daphne's advice and look after myself more. :-)

The choice of setting for *Of Vines and Victims* came about following a library talk I gave some time ago at Benalla Library. There was plenty of encouragement from the attendees to include Benalla, which has proved to be a delightful setting. I have to acknowledge each of them for their support. The winery is purely from my imagination as I've not had to pleasure yet of visiting any which are close to the town. I have taken small liberties with some descriptions and also extended the time anyone is permitted to camp on the little island.

Finally, I'd like to mention my father-in-law, a gentle and kind man who has called me 'doll' on more than one occasion.

Thank you always to my family and to the friends who never let me give up – Michelle M, Susan M, and Heather R.

www.ingramcontent.com/pod-product-compliance
Lightning Source LLC
Chambersburg PA
CBHW011557190726
48287CB00010B/2942